RAFFERTY'S RULE NUMBER THIRTY-NINE: SMITING THE WICKED SOUNDS BIBLICAL, BUT MOSTLY IT'S GOOD CLEAN FUN.

"Okay."I opened a desk drawer and reached inside it. Red and Junior were two full beats late. My hand was coming out of the drawer before their hands started under their suit coats.

I smiled at them and held up the paper clip from the drawer. They tried to turn their hand movements into scratches while I twiddled the paper clip around in the bowl of my pipe and removed a clot of horrible black gunk.

Now we all knew were we stood. I didn't (well, probably didn't) have a gun in the desk and they did have guns under their coats. There were three of them, including Hadley, and they were standing. I was alone and seated.

But I was me and they were them, so I made the odds about even. . . .

RAFFERTY: POOR DEAD CRICKET

W. Glenn Duncan

FAWCETT GOLD MEDAL • NEW YORK

A Fawcett Gold Medal Book
Published by Ballantine Books
Copyright © 1988 by W. Glenn Duncan

Library of Congress Catalog Card Number: 87-92136

ISBN 0-449-13325-7

Manufactured in the United States of America

First Edition: July 1988

This book is for my best friend, Val.

Portion of a handwritten journal kept by Norwood A. Kempler

. . . down. That was not nice. If i knew a girl, i wudn't fight with her, no way hose-A!!

8's jungle is shaped like a heart. It can't grow like that. She must trim it or something.

19 had 11 in for lunch. Boy, is 11 a dummy!! He didn't even try! If he knew 19 like i do, he'd sure try, you bet he wud!

The 37s did it again today. She 37 wore her lacy blue thing that makes her big ones stick out. She really liked it when he 37 put . . .

CHAPTER ONE

The address Winchester had given me turned out to be a storefront office on Elm Street. Deep Ellum, they call it, and it's an area, really, a special place on the seedy edge of the inner city. It used to be bad news, but it's coming back now. New shops and fresh paint and classy window arrangements. Gentrification, thy name is Deep Ellum.

Winchester's headquarters had a twenty-five foot frontage. It wasn't as fancy as the commercial shops, but it had been fixed up some. The frames around the plate glass windows were freshly painted, and centered on the expanse of each window there were identical signs. THE GREEN ARMY, they said, in khaki lettering like a military stencil.

Inside, it was bright but crowded. Most of the building was one big room crammed with ancient desks and tables. It hummed with that peculiarly earnest enthusiasm found in organizations staffed by volunteers. A dozen or so people—mostly young, mostly hairy—beavered away industriously. They stuffed envelopes, fed mimeograph machines, and muttered into telephones. They were all very serious about whatever it was they were doing.

There was a scarred desk just inside the front door. Long ago someone had painted it an unfortunate shade of green. A girl in her early or mid-twenties sat there, leaning on sharp elbows, talking into a telephone. She was very thin, with a narrow face and a red fuzzy hairdo that seemed a shoe-in for Permanent-of-The-Month. She had big eyes, too, and good teeth, and quite possibly a nice smile. As it happened, she wasn't smiling then.

"I don't like the sound of that, Mike," she said into the phone. "Why won't he show you the environmental-impact statement?"

She sighed and tugged at her tightly coiled hair as she listened. Finally she said, "Well, okay then, let's lean on him. You tell that turkey we get a copy of that statement today or we'll have two hundred demonstrators in front of his crummy company at eight o'clock tomorrow." She listened again, then smiled tightly. "You got that right. So long."

She nodded to herself as she clunked the receiver onto its cradle, then looked up at me. "Yes?" she asked sweetly.

"I'm Rafferty," I said. "I have an appointment with Winchester."

"Oh, right. Hang on, I'll see if he's free."

I stopped her before she got away. "What's the hassle?" I nodded at her telephone.

"That? Oh, a tannery wants to increase its effluent discharge rate. Nothing big, really, but we're keeping an eye on it."

"No kidding."

She laughed. It suited her. "Oh, I was only bluffing about the demonstration. You have to act tough with these companies or they'll walk all over you. They have all the advantages, you know."

I nodded seriously. "Oh, I know."

She looked at me strangely. "I'll tell Dr. Winchester you're here," she said, and she walked toward the back of the large room, dodging through the maze of jumbled desks.

I waited under an air-conditioning vent that struggled uselessly against the crowded, stuffy room. A few of the workers glanced at me, then went back to saving the world.

The skinny redhead knocked on a closed door at the back of the room, immediately opened it, and stuck her head inside. A moment later she turned and waved me forward, into the tiny office and the large presence of The Green Army's commanding officer.

"Hi! I'm Jim Winchester," he boomed. "Hey, thanks very much for coming so quickly. This is terrific!"

Winchester was thirty, maybe thirty-two, lean and athletic looking, with a long face. His big brown eyes had thick lashes. He was clean shaven, which put him in the minority in his organization, and he wore a suit, which made him unique.

"Here, have a seat. Sorry about the mess. We're pretty cramped, as you can see."

I could see. His office was no more than six feet by ten, maybe even a touch smaller. His desk and chair, a wooden visitor's chair, and two file cabinets almost filled it. Reports, papers, and books were piled on every level surface.

Winchester closed a file with a flourish, set it aside, and leaned forward over his desktop. He clasped his hands together and served up a broad, confident smile with bucketloads of eye contact.

He reminded me of a used-car salesman who once unloaded an eight-year-old Falcon on me.

"So," he said, "you're Rafferty, the private investigator!"

He seemed so proud he'd gotten it right, it was a shame not to preen for him. I passed up the opportunity anyway.

"I'm Rafferty, *a* private investigator, yes. And you're Winchester. Did I hear the girl say Dr. Winchester?"

He gave me an aw-shucks smile so perfect he must have practiced it in his bathroom mirror. "Well, that's right, but since I don't practice medicine, I rarely use the honorific."

I nodded at him, just another man of the world. "I know how it is, Jim. I hardly ever wear my Sharpshooter badge anymore."

He either ignored that or didn't hear it. "Too much work to do, Rafferty. I simply cannot afford the luxury of a practice." Winchester shook his head thoughtfully. "I first became involved in environmental and ecological issues in medical school. Lord only knows how I found time for outside activities during internship and residency, but I did, somehow. And then, when it was time to set up shop, I realized I didn't want to practice medicine. So I founded The Green Army instead." He shook his boyish head again, in case I had somehow missed the wonder of it all.

"Yeah. Well, what can I do for—"

"And The Green Army has become my life, Rafferty, my entire life. This is not our only office, of course. I still work out of here for sentimental reasons. This is where it all began." He let out a wry smile. "We've come a long way. More than thirty branches. Over twelve thousand financial contributors nationwide. Twice as many volunteer workers. Plus wide support from the community at large during our campaigns exposing vital issues." He mustered a dedicated, serious look. "The American people are growing ever more conscious of the need to protect their environment and preserve the delicate balance of ecology before it's too late."

"On the phone you said you wanted to hire me. Could we talk about that?"

"Umm, well, yes, I do have a job for you. I want you to prove the Dormac-Chaffee Corporation murdered Cricket Dawes." Winchester smiled confidently, with the sort of look a British general on the Late Late Movie uses when he says "Carry on then, there's a good chap."

I sighed. "Well, we're getting somewhere, I suppose. I know who Dormac-Chaffee is. I think. They operate some nuclear whatzit out past Garland, don't they?"

"Yes. It's a reprocessing plant. They recover uranium and plutonium from spent fuel rods. Very dangerous. It's a scandal how they operate."

"Oh, I'm sure," I said. "So, presumably they're the bad guys. But who—besides you and me—are the good guys? And who is Cricket Dawes?"

"Cricket was killed last Friday evening, at the apartment building where she lives. Lived. Didn't you hear about it?"

"I remember something about a woman killed by a mugger. That may be the one. I hate to tell you this, but I don't cry myself to sleep over the Dallas crime statistics."

From the way Winchester looked at me, I knew I wouldn't be receiving an invitation to join The Green Army. Lack of social conscience, the committee would say, if they had a committee to say things like that.

Winchester blew out a long breath, gave another slow, sad shake of his head and told me the big secret. "Cricket—her real name was Sandra—anyway, Cricket Dawes was a Dormac-Chaffee employee. She worked there from 1981 until, um, Friday. For the last year and a half, Cricket was assistant to the head of Quality Control and Materiel Security. And during that time, she became deeply disturbed about the appalling safety conditions and the total lack of concern shown by the money grubbers operating that evil plant."

I wondered if Winchester realized he sounded like a recruiting poster for the Orange County Anti-Nuke Marxist Feminist Video Unit.

"What appalling safety conditions?" I said.

"Increasing radiation levels, improper decontamination, sloppy inventories of radioactive materials, temporary workers used as guinea pigs; that sort of thing."

"Oh, I see. That sort of thing."

"Don't scoff. Suppose the inventories *are* wrong. Suppose radioactive materials are being stolen from that plant."

"Yeah, that'll do it. And you think she was murdered because of what she knew?"

Winchester set his jaw. "I am morally *certain* she was murdered because she intended to reveal the truth about Dormac-Chaffee."

"Through The Green Army," I said.

"Certainly. Cricket told us about the operations at the plant and I arranged the press contact for her. Friday night, Cricket planned to turn over documentary evidence."

"Where?"

"At her apartment on Gaston Avenue. I picked up Sam Burrell from the *Star-Democrat* and took him to Cricket's place. When we arrived, the parking lot was full of police. Cricket was lying beside her car. Dead."

"Have you followed this up with the cops?"

"Not very far," he said. "They think it was a holdup or attempted rape that went wrong."

I said, "Did you tell them your suspicions about Dormac-Chaffee?"

Winchester pursed his lips and shook his head. "Why? Without any proof, all I would do is warn Dormac-Chaffee and invite a libel suit. Not that I mind a libel suit, particularly; that would give me a chance to expose their operation. But I think we can do better. So I called you."

"Okay. Now exactly what was the 'documentary evidence' she said she had?"

"Dormac-Chaffee files."

"And you assume Dormac-Chaffee recovered them, right?"

Winchester frowned. "I'm not sure. There is a slight chance Cricket hid them in her apartment. You should definitely check there. The problem is, I understand Cricket planned to take the files Friday afternoon and return them this morning, after Burrell had examined them over the weekend. And after I had photocopied them. So she probably had them in her car. She was killed as she arrived home from work."

"Okay. Now, 'files' can mean anything from annual budgets to lunchroom purchase orders. Do you know what is supposed to be involved here?"

"Only in general terms. Apparently they indicate a shortage of radioactive materials, but I don't know how much is missing or from which department or the date when the shortage was first noticed. And Cricket told us about reports detailing high radioactivity levels, but I don't know the values or the location of the leak. Or leaks." He shrugged and raised his hands like the Pope at Easter. "How can I go public without hard data?"

I didn't much like the way he worried about the files and treated the girl's death as a minor annoyance. "Life's a bitch, all right. And you don't know whether this Cricket Dawes actually lifted the files or not. They could still be at the plant. And her death could be exactly what the cops say it was."

Winchester shook his head doggedly. "I refuse to accept that."

This time I shrugged. "We'll see. I'll poke around, and we'll see."

Winchester slipped out of his somber mode and back into his gee-whiz phase. "Okay? You'll do it?"

"Sure. No guarantees, though."

"Oh, this is great! Just find me some evidence, even circumstantial if it's good enough, and I'll go public with it. Get the files if you can." He held up one hand when I grimaced. "I realize you may not be able to get the files. If not, okay. I'll go without them if I absolutely have to."

I was pretty good. I didn't say anything about Winchester's cavalier attitude. Well, I was working for him now. Which brought to mind . . .

"About my fee, I—"

Winchester coughed gently. "Uh, I hope you'll take into account the vital public interest involved here. In setting the fee, I mean, and perhaps you'd be willing to—"

I shook my head. "The daily rate is the same for everybody. Two hundred a day, plus expenses. Three days' pay up front."

Winchester struck a pose. He pursed his lips, which made him look odd because then his eyes didn't match the rest of his face. His mouth frowned: *How crass and commercial you are, you misguided innocent,* while his eyes twinkled: *You can't blame me for trying.*

"Can't you send a bill afterward?" he asked.

"No. Rafferty's Rule Number Thirteen: Get the money up front."

Actually, Rule Thirteen only applies to committees and obvious deadbeats, but I didn't tell him that. Instead, I gave him my best disarming smile. Hilda Gardner says my disarming smile resembles a cretin suffering gas pains, but I sometimes use it anyway.

"You see," I said to Winchester, "sometimes things don't work out the way people expect. Then they get owly and don't want to pay me for my time. And it's too hard to collect from fund-raising committees and do-gooder groups. So I take six hundred up front."

Winchester's eyes were no longer amused. "The Green Army is not a do-gooder group!"

I let that one go by without comment.

He tried twenty seconds of cool brown eyes and drumming fingers, but I was so tough I withstood that, too. Finally he sighed and said, "All right. I'll get you a check."

"Fine. And I'll need details—addresses and such—before I go."

Half an hour later, with The Green Army's check in my wallet and three full pages in my notebook, I fought my way out of the crowded front office. As I reached for the door handle, someone called out, "Hey, Rafferty! Hang on a second."

The thin redhead angled across the room toward me. Behind her the volunteer workers looked up from their tasks. A shaggy envelope stuffer grinned.

The redhead stopped beside me, grabbed my left buttock, and kneaded it like a suspect melon. "Play along," she said. "This is winning me twenty bucks, believe it or not."

Across the room, the envelope stuffer laughed and raised his arms in surrender.

Redhead let go of my butt and smiled cheerfully. "Hey, thanks for being a good sport," she said, and turned to walk away. She stopped after the first step, though, and looked back over her shoulder. "Nice buns, too. Especially for a guy your age."

Then she strutted away, getting an extra inch into each swing of her slim hips.

There wasn't much to say to the back of her head and a dozen smirking faces, so I left.

Outside, on the sidewalk, when it was too late, I thought of seventeen snappy comebacks I could have used but didn't.

Sometimes forty seems so damned old.

CHAPTER TWO

"Winchester is pulling your chain," said The Grape. "*Thirty* branches? He's really flipped this time."

The Grape's real name was Siedles. He pronounced it seedless, so I called him The Grape. He didn't like that much, but he put up with it.

"*Doctor* James Winchester," The Grape said. "Boy dilettante." He shook his head. "The people you have to put up with in this racket . . ."

The Grape had been one of the original Texas conservationists, way back in the days when the general feeling was that conservationists were only a "buncha nuts go around talkin' to trees and bugs and stuff." Then the hippies came along, and they all liked talking to trees and bugs and stuff, so The Grape fit right in. In fact, he still looked right for the Age of Aquarius. At least, he looked right from the neck up. Imagine Woody Allen with a bushy steel-wool wig. In a six-hundred-dollar suit. And Gucci loafers.

"The Green Army is strictly local," The Grape said. "Hey, Winchester might have two cousins in Detroit and he calls them the Michigan branch, but that's as far as it goes." The Grape scooped a small handful of macadamia nuts out of a silver bowl, chewed them, and washed them down with Heineken's from a tissue-thin pilsner glass.

The Grape had an unusual background. He'd been part of

the ecology movement for so long that no one could doubt his expertise, but that didn't mean he was easy to understand.

The Grape's transformation from run-of-the-mill ecologist to someone special began ten or twelve years earlier. The Grape took on an oil company, and there was a long, bitter campaign. The fight was all about potential foreshore pollution down on the Gulf, but I was more intrigued by the courage The Grape showed. You just don't argue with oil companies in Texas without picking up scars.

And The Grape picked up scars. It wasn't a single-handed fight on his part, but damn near, and The Grape was both prime mover and prime target. He was accused of everything from stifling the economy to promoting free love in kindergartens. The papers were full of that drivel. The TV news, too, but The Grape hung tight, and he kept fighting and eventually he won.

For six months, The Grape was the darling of every conservationist group in the Southwest. They loved him. He was the all-conquering hero. The Grape could do no wrong.

Wait for it.

A year after his antipollution triumph, The Grape endorsed a plan to build public housing apartments on a site to be cleared of trees and animals.

"Well, what else can I do?" he told me at the time. "Texas is up to here in bois d'arc trees, the racoons will be moved by the Wildlife Department, and the new housing will get some people off the street and under a roof for the first time in years. I mean, for crying out loud, you have to be *logical*!"

Overnight The Grape became environmentally suspect. Well, not totally. There were one or two groups who agreed with him, but they weren't very effusive about it. Most of the ecology movement simply ignored the issue. Out on the lunatic fringe, a few people stomped and screamed and sent strange letters.

That's how I met The Grape. I did a week of protection work for him before we mutually agreed that I wasn't needed. Anyone who wrote with crayon and misspelled "castrate" was unlikely to raise the bus fare from El Paso to Dallas, let alone carry out his lurid threat.

But the environmentalists weren't the only people confused about The Grape. After the apartment kerfuffle, a go-getter with dollar signs for eyes assumed The Grape had embraced rampant capitalism. Go-getter never quite understood what happened when The Grape listened and nodded, then scuttled his pet project, a weird and not-so-wonderful scheme involving—if I remember correctly—a fleet of two hundred rental houseboats on White Rock Lake.

But The Grape went along with another project the following month—even though somebody would profit by it—because it would benefit people without unduly harming the environment.

The business community and the ecology movement scratched their collective heads and asked simultaneously: "How can you figure a guy like that?"

Eventually The Grape decided that, as long he was burdened with an overpowering sense of principle, he might as well make a buck out of it. So he started charging for consultant work. And if he liked your idea, he might endorse it, but he would charge for that, too, because he needed the loot to finance the opposition campaign if the next project you proposed turned out to be bad news.

The Grape called it the Robin Hood Theory of Economic Rationalism.

Surprisingly, that approach had proved just go-to-hell enough to work. So now The Grape—with his integrity still intact—made a lot of money by being himself. Beat that for a job description.

All of which explained why The Grape and I were sitting in his office snacking on Heineken's and macadamias in crystal and silver instead of Thunderbird and raisins in bottle and bag.

"Winchester calls his group The Green Army," I said. "What is that, a branch of Greenpeace or something?"

The Grape snorted. "Are you kidding? Greenpeace wouldn't let Winchester carry one of their signs, let alone have any affiliation with him. They're serious; he's a turkey."

The Grape crunched another macadamia. "Tell you the truth, I think he even stole that Green Army name. I'd swear I've heard that, or something like it, before. And I think that group was pretty straight."

I nodded. "And Winchester's not straight?"

The Grape twirled his forefinger in a climbing, swirling motion.

"Would you call Winchester's group small-time?"

" 'Puny' is a good word," The Grape said. "See also 'minuscule' and 'irrelevant.' "

"Why, Big Jim done told me he's got twelve thousand members. Looked me right in the eye when he said it, too, so's I'd know he warn't kiddin' me."

The Grape grimaced. "Don't do that shit-kicker dialect, Rafferty. You're terrible at it." He crunched another handful of macadamias. "Winchester's a flake," he said. "And desperate. He's hurting for a campaign."

"Come on," I said, "you make him sound like a third-rate ad agency."

The Grape shrugged. "The ecology movement isn't immune from crackpot members. Why should we be somehow holier than doctors or plumbers or librarians or—" He pointed at me. "—or hired thugs? Actually, if you think about it, all those other groups have to have a license or special training. Anyone can be an environmentalist by simply declaring themselves one. Who else can do that?"

"Politicians," I said, "but that only reinforces your point."

The Grape drained his beer and went to his office refrigerator for two more bottles. "One thing. Just because a flake can be an environmentalist, that doesn't mean every environmentalist is a flake. Right?"

He waited until I nodded to show I'd fully grasped that concept before he handed me my second beer. The Grape looked like a wimp, but he could be tough at times.

The Grape said, "Okay. Now, about flakes and campaigns—"

"And things that go bump in the night."

"Don't interrupt. I'm being serious. When I said Winchester needed a campaign, that shows how much of a flake he is. It's an ego trip for him.''

I dove into the second Heineken's and came up smiling. I said, ''Sounds like a lot of work to see your name in the paper every once in a while.''

''Don't you believe it,'' said The Grape. ''You'd be surprised what— Look at it this way. Sometime or another, in some organization or another, you've seen a person finagle and wheedle, maybe actually lie and cheat, just for the personal satisfaction of taking over or influencing that group. Everyone has seen that drive for power. It's not about money or property, it's about power and the willing compliance of a subordinate group. C'mon, Rafferty. It happens every day in clubs and trade associations and community service organizations and—''

''Yeah, yeah,'' I said. ''I know what you mean now.''

He nodded. ''Okay, then. That's why Winchester needs a campaign. And he better get hot. From what I hear, The Green Army is about to fall apart.''

''A visit with you always tops up my cynicism, Grape.''

''Tough. Think of how I feel, being on the same side as that jerk, when and if he remembers to jump onto the bandwagon.''

''Enough with the psychology, Grape. Let's talk about glowing in the dark.'' I told him about Dormac-Chaffee, Cricket Dawes, and what Winchester thought was going on.

The Grape frowned and sucked his teeth. ''That's a tough one. The nuclear power industry scares the hell out of me. So. I cannot objectively advise you on that subject. However, two thoughts come to mind. First, the information may not be legitimate. It's only hearsay so far, and personally, I'd look up at the sky if Winchester told me it was daytime. Which brings up the second thought: you probably won't get paid.''

''Got his check in my wallet.''

The Grape raised his eyebrows. ''Hmm. Even so, cash it before you put any more work on the meter.''

I toasted him with my glass. ''I intend to, but thanks for the tip.''

The Grape gave me his fish-eye look. "You always check up on your clients?"

"Almost always. The situation is covered by a Rafferty's Rule: In one way or another, every client lies."

"I should have guessed. Which number Rule is that?"

"Twenty-seven, I think. Grape, can you put me onto anyone who works—or has worked—at Dormac-Chaffee? I don't know zip about what they do out there. And I'd like a backup opinion on what Dawes told Winchester. Whoops, what Winchester *says* Dawes told him."

"You're learning," The Grape said. "Let me work on that and get back to you." He checked the time on a gold wrist watch the size of a dinner plate and the thickness of a dime. "Now go away, will you? Believe it or not, I have better things to do than feed you beer and tell tales out of school."

The bank had the bottom two floors of a brushed-metal-and-smoked-glass prism on Commerce Street. I suppose the offices on the second floor might have been all right, but down in the lobby, the decor was early science-fiction movie. I kept expecting Michael Rennie to appear in a silver jumpsuit and ask to be taken to my leader.

Most of the tellers were women in bright, chaste uniforms that made them look like fundamentalist chorus girls. To judge by the facial expressions, several of them had the flu.

The people in my line were lucky, though, and I eventually found myself facing a handsome gal about thirty-five, with long red fingernails and a ready smile. But when she did her modern banking *tappa-tappa-whir-click* number, she lost the smile.

"Oh, I'm sorry, sir. That account has insufficient funds to cover this check."

Somehow it didn't surprise me. "They said they would make a deposit this afternoon," I lied. "Could you check on whether they've . . . ?"

"Oh. Just a moment."

She asked someone something, poked more buttons, and came up with better news. She whacked the check with a rubber stamp, scribbled on it, and dealt out the cash. "You were right. It just came through." She giggled. "And here it goes out again." Then, the obligatory Texas farewell. "You come back, y'hear?"

"Sure," I said absently. If a six-hundred-dollar check meant a special trip to the bank, The Green Army sliced its finances pretty close to the bone.

CHAPTER THREE

Even with Winchester's cash advance in my pocket, it wasn't quite clear sailing. The Mustang went through one of its hard-starting fits, and I was late getting out to McKinney Avenue.

I double-parked the Mustang in front of Gardner's Antiques and headed for the door. The dead bolt snicked closed as I crossed the sidewalk. Then Ramon, Hilda's head salesman, smirked at me while he slowly pulled down the long shade on the glass door.

Ramon sure knew how to hold a grudge; it had been at least four months since I'd teased him about those blue velvet jeans.

Hilda's red BMW nosed out of the narrow alley beside the shop, so I ignored Ramon and trotted up the sidewalk.

Hilda hadn't seen me coming; she was peering up the street waiting for a break in the traffic. She wore sunglasses, which unfortunately hid her dark eyes, but there was still the way the sun fell on her cheek and the curly mass of her black hair and the small pink perfection of her earlobe and—

She started to pull out onto the road. I stopped mooning over her just in time to slap the BMW's trunk lid. Hilda jammed on the brakes with a sharp little squeak and looked around. She found me smiling at her.

"Rafferty! You startled—"

16

"Tell me, my sweet. Throughout these endless hours when we're separated, do you find yourself longing for the feel of my strong arms around your trembling body?"

She frowned, deep in mock thought. "Well, if I ever do, I'll certainly give you a call."

"Ouch. Sorry I'm late, babe. You still have that meeting tonight?"

"Business before pleasure, big guy. Want to wait for me at my place? I should be back around ten-thirty or eleven." Hilda wore a dark summer-weight dress with a high neck and a fairly severe cut; part of her business-lady wardrobe.

"Maybe. I think I'll work tonight, too. Why do you wear clothes with no neckline? Here I am, standing beside the car with a clear height advantage, and I can't see down the front of your dress."

Hilda grinned. "Your memory's good enough to tide you over. What's this 'work tonight' business? That insurance thing?"

"No. A little case that came up today. Short one, I guarantee. We are definitely off to San Antonio for the weekend."

Hilda gave me that look.

"Promise, babe. I'll tell you all about it later, but basically the client sees boogeymen and murder-most-foul in what was probably just a simple mugging. I'll wrap it up in three days. Maybe two."

"If you say so. See you tonight?"

I squatted beside the BMW. Our faces were on the same level then, and I kissed the tip of her nose. Great nose.

"I hope so," I said. "It all depends. If I have to do a burglary, it might get to be too late. You wouldn't start without me, would you?"

"You never know."

She kissed me then, so I kissed her back, and we went on like that for a while, until someone in a silver Mercedes honked the horn at my double-parked Mustang. Hilda and I came out of our daze; she drove off with a laugh and a wave, and I stood there smiling.

I waved at the Mercedes to relax and noticed it wasn't as late as I'd thought. Ramon had unlocked the front door again;

he was bowing and scraping good-bye to a middle-aged couple lugging an ornate gilt clock.

When the couple turned away, Ramon looked at me. He slowly wet the tip of his finger and made a one-point-for-me gesture on an invisible wall. The guy in the Mercedes honked again and yelled something surly.

So what? How could I get angry after necking with Hilda? I climbed into the Mustang and drove away laughing.

CHAPTER FOUR

I left the Mustang parked on a side street two blocks away and walked down Gaston Avenue to the apartment building where Cricket Dawes had lived and died. The place was called Casa Cahuenga, which seemed awfully cutesy to me, but what the hell, I didn't live there.

A wall of mailboxes out front told me there were thirty-four apartments and that S. Dawes lived in number twenty-four.

The two-story building was a hollow rectangle with all the apartments facing inward toward a courtyard that was half lawn and half swimming pool. The upper level of apartments opened onto a walkway that ran all the way around the inside of the rectangle. There were four stairways, one in each corner.

Casa Cahuenga was probably fifteen years old. It seemed well maintained and clean. The place was a little down-market for genuine grade-A yuppies; I guessed it drew a young singles crowd still working on the deposit for their first BMW.

The exact socioeconomic background of the residents didn't bother me too much. Dress for success, they say, and I was prepared for a wide range of sneaky activities. I wore a dark blue polo shirt; the only one I own with an alligator on the chest. I wore jeans that were faded just enough to be trendy or old, depending on who was judging. Plus a pair of two-year-old but rarely worn Frye boots and a fake-gold neck chain Hilda had once given me as a joke.

The plan was to put out enough confusing signals that I could slide into almost any group Casa Cahuenga could muster.

I had lockpicks in my hip pocket and a blackjack in my right boot, too, but I wasn't signaling with those. A nice fellow like me wouldn't want to fall in with the wrong crowd.

Nine o'clock on a summery Monday night was a good time to go visiting at the Casa Cahuenga. There was a fair crowd in the courtyard, most of them in and around the pool.

A woman in a green bathing suit was swimming laps. Noisily. Besides the splashes, she made explosive little snorts like an angry seal. A husky blond guy in his early twenties had a girl in a yellow bikini backed up against one of the pool ladders. He had one hand on each ladder upright. She was between his arms, trapped and loving it. They nuzzled each other and didn't look up when I walked past.

There were also ten or twelve people lounging on folding chairs and chaises around the shallow end of the pool. They looked up when I coughed and mumbled, "Uh, excuse me . . ."

I had decided to open with a humble but earnest, down-home gambit. Apply liberally and modify as necessary.

Humble, earnest, and down-home earned me a dozen blank stares, all automatically playing make-the-outsider-uncomfortable. Strange game, that one. I often wondered why it was so popular.

I scuffed one boot toe on the flagstone paving and let my eyes drop. I thought about throwing in an "aw, shucks," but I didn't.

"Looking for Cricket Dawes," I said. "She told me the apartment number, but I forgot."

One guy with a chestful of curly hair slapped his forehead with the heel of his hand and made a village idiot face. "Duh," he said, "boy, oh, boy, am I—"

Then a chunky girl with short brown hair came down on my side with an anguished, "Oh, no, you mean you haven't heard?"

After that it became a contest to see who could tell me about Cricket the fastest. They all talked at the same time, then took a breath while I trotted out a story about meeting Cricket a few weeks ago and just getting back into town, and no, I didn't know, and damn, what's the world coming to anyway?

The chunky girl moved right on to "Jimmy, get him a beer" and "Come sit down and we'll tell you all about it."

And so they did.

At first, they seemed to want to tell it one more time, but then they wore themselves out. After all, they'd been chewing it over and over for the past three days. They should have been getting sick of the taste of it by then.

It wasn't long before the group began to shrink.

A pair of rawboned cowboy types left first. The couple in the pool climbed out and drifted away to an apartment in the back. A Southwest Airlines stew departed in a flurry of long smooth legs and carefully tangled hair. A Trivial Pursuit challenge took away three or four more.

The floodlights around the pool clicked off at ten-thirty. By then there were only three of us left: Bev, the chunky girl; Stuart, a very, very serious SMU law student; and good old R. J. Drew, the traveling shooting-iron salesman from Odessa, by golly gosh.

R. J. Drew was me. And I didn't like me very much then. Why had I bothered to skulk in here and lie to these people?

My only answer to that was the streaker's defense: it seemed like a good idea at the time. And I did have a job to do, so . . .

"Why do you suppose she was killed?"

Stuart shrugged. "Robbery, I'd say. Her purse was missing."

"Umm. Well, I still don't understand how she could get mugged and killed in broad daylight without anybody seeing it happen."

"You'd have to know this place, R. J. Everybody works. It's like a wasteland during the day. Right, Bev?"

"Oh, sure," she said. "When I had the flu, it was so quiet it was spooky." She screwed her round gamine face up in thought. "Let's see now, Becky is the only girl who doesn't work. But Vince—he works the morning shift at the post office—gets home about three, and they usually spend the afternoon in their apartment." She giggled cheerfully.

"The couple who were in the pool," Stuart said quietly. "They've only been living together for a month."

We sophisticated gentlemen nodded solemnly.

I said, "Cricket was found a little before five, but you're telling me it could have happened anytime that afternoon. It just doesn't sound right, Stuart."

"Theoretically it's possible. Cricket's parking slot is in the back row. Steve Margolin's slot is in front of Cricket's, and Steve has a big camper on his pickup. It blocks the view. So far as I am able to determine, at least three people passed within thirty feet of where she lay in the hour before she was found. If Steve hadn't gone out to his camper, she might have lain there unseen even longer."

He stopped talking when the Spanish-style porch lights along the walkways went out. Time clock or an early-to-bed manager?

About half the draped windows around the courtyard glowed, but where we sat the only light came from the underwater fixtures in the pool. I wondered if they left them on all night to keep the drunks from falling in.

The low lights caught Stuart under the chin and made him look old and pontifical. I was about to prompt him, but before I could speak, he went on.

"On the other hand, there is a certain amount of traffic through the alley that runs behind the parking area. Garbage trucks use it. Milk trucks use it. So do kids on bicycles, the occasional bum, and of course, the residents here. Logically, someone *had* to see her before too long. So perhaps it did happen just before Steve Margolin found her."

"Hey, look, Stuart, I don't want to cut down any of your friends, but what about this guy Margolin? He found her, he says. But could he have done it?"

Stuart looked at Bev, who shrugged. He thought for a moment, then said, "No, I seriously doubt it. Margolin is . . . well, I suppose you could call him our resident aging hippy.

He thinks he's still a flower child. I doubt he spends more than ten minutes a day not stoned to the eyeballs. And he gets happy, dreamy stoned, not violent. And finally, a person I trust saw him go out, then come running back a few seconds later. Oh, and Margolin is *not* a friend of mine."

"Okay. Sorry."

Bev chipped in with: "Hey, you guys, I feel terrible about Cricket and all, but I'm really not so worried about *how* it happened. I am scared to death because it happened at all! I mean, who's gonna be next? Me? No way! Why, I spent fifteen minutes sitting in my car today waiting for someone else to get home. I came in with that animal Mitch Lovell rather than walk fifty feet by myself. I'm talking *terror* here, guys."

Stuart pulled a sour face. "You are overreacting, Bev. The incidence of random violence is very small when measured against the total population. And, statistically, the chance of another similar incident here is infinitesimal."

Bev turned to me. "Don't you just love it when he talks like that? I swear there's a special course at SMU law. Modern Communications and Polysyllabic Bullshit 203." She jumped up and ruffled Stuart's hair. "Only kidding, baby. Hey, listen, you two. I have a very important job for you. Sit here and watch me walk to my apartment, okay? If the phantom grabs me, call the cops or the army or somebody, and come a-running."

"Sure, Bev. Good night."

"Sleep well," said Stuart.

"Sleep?" Bev said. "While the monster walks? I don't hold out much hope."

She waggled her fingers at us, smiled, and walked around the pool. Stuart and I watched her go to a corner of the courtyard and disappear up a concrete stairway. A few seconds later, she emerged on the second floor. We scraped and dragged our chairs around to follow her as she went along the upper walkway and unlocked a door. She stepped into the doorway, switched on a light, made an exaggerated mime of checking for intruders, then waved at us again and closed the door.

Stuart sighed and said, "Funny."

"What is?"

"Us. You and me. We both knew there was absolutely no chance of Bev running into trouble between here and her door, yet we sat here like mute bodyguards and watched her every second. This sort of thing is hard on people. It warps their outlook." He shook his head wearily. "Well, I'm off, too. Mock court tomorrow, and I'm no more ready than usual."

We shook hands and parted. As I went out through the front walkway, I looked back and saw him standing by a ground-floor apartment watching me. I waved and strolled out, whistling loudly like innocent, aboveboard country boy R. J. Drew might do.

I felt a little frayed around the edges after lying to innocent people I liked. I told myself I wasn't doing anything really low and despicable, like writing political campaign speeches, but that didn't cheer me up much.

Two hours later I went back and burgled the place.

CHAPTER FIVE

I stood in the black stairwell and listened.

Bev was right to be worried. Security at Casa Cahuenga had more loopholes than a used-car warranty. The alley Stuart had mentioned ran behind the building, parallel with Gaston Avenue. A narrow driveway connected that alley with Gaston. I had walked down the alley, then down the driveway, hugging the building. Finally I stepped into a side entrance. I had never been exposed to view from any apartment window or from the courtyard.

The architect who designed Casa Cahuenga must have moonlighted as a burglar.

When I was sure there was no one moving around, I climbed the stairs and ghosted along the walkway toward Cricket's apartment. Well, I ghosted as well as a guy my size wearing boots can ghost. It was good enough.

Number twenty-four was halfway along the short western side of the building. I thought of Bev again when the cheap and nasty lock popped open as soon as I inserted two lockpicks and stirred a little.

Shazam. I was inside.

The drapes were closed, but I left the lights off anyway. I had a flashlight from the Mustang; I used that as I strolled through the apartment, not looking seriously yet, just getting the feel of the place.

The front door opened into the living room–dining area. A tiny kitchen and serving counter were tucked in one corner. A short hallway—bathroom left and closet right—led to the single bedroom.

The furniture was apartment-motel-trade standard, with hard, knobbly fabrics and no real wood anywhere. It matched the drapes and carpets well enough to tell me this was a furnished apartment. I'd have to dig a little to learn anything about Cricket Dawes as a person.

The first thing I wanted to see was her kitchen calendar. Women use calendars on kitchen walls like men use desk diaries or appointment books; real slice-of-life stuff for the discriminating snooper.

Cricket's calendar had a big picture of a west Texas sunset and no end of news: she was going to miss her mother's birthday next week, her rent was due on the first of each month and her car payment on the twentieth, someone named Donna had an anniversary (of what?) coming up, and Cricket's last period started nine days ago.

There were a few other bits and pieces on the pages for past and future months but nothing that looked particularly promising. There were several scraps of paper attached to the calendar picture with a big red plastic squeeze clip. I tugged them loose and went through them. One was a note of Winchester's name and phone number. The handwriting was large and swirly, like the calendar jottings. The rest was typical household detritus: credit card receipts, dental appointment reminders, supermarket coupons, things like that.

The little kitchen was tidy, possibly because it wasn't big enough to afford disorder. There was a spice rack on the wall. The counter held a toaster, a food processor, and a pine breadbox with half a loaf of white bread lightly dusted with mold.

I'd tried that brand of bread myself; you got a lot of sandwiches out of one loaf, but it had no discernible taste, and the texture was like foam rubber. Cheap foam rubber.

There was no dust or dirt showing, but the kitchen counter had a very slightly gritty feel when I dragged my fingertips across it. That seemed about right for a place that had been locked up since Friday morning.

The refrigerator and kitchen cabinets told me a bit more about Cricket Dawes. She liked strawberry yogurt and bought thick T-bones one at a time. She ate English muffins, sugar-coated breakfast cereal, and whipped margarine. She smoked Virginia Slims. There were four packs left in the carton.

The dishes were everyday single-girl stuff in bright colors with a simple geometric pattern and a vaguely Mexican look. They were apparently used with a set of quilted place mats. One of the cheery plates, with egg yolk hardened on it, was racked in the dishwasher. A small plate (toast?), a juice glass, and a coffee cup also waited patiently to be washed.

There were two good crystal wineglasses but no wine in the current inventory. Instead, a half-empty bottle of Stolichnaya and an unopened gift box of Jim Beam shared a lower shelf corner.

There was no garbage. A yellow kitchen bin had been lined with a clean plastic bag. She'd probably taken the last batch out with her on Friday morning.

The dining area was simply the space between the kitchen service counter and the wall. It had a plain table, four chairs, and all the charm of a concrete block.

Going through Cricket's apartment was boring and tedious. As usual, I felt like a grocery store clerk taking inventory; the task was boring as hell, but I couldn't afford to be sloppy because I didn't know what was there and what was missing.

Back to work, Rafferty.

There were a few personal touches in the living room. Vases of now-droopy flowers sat on end tables flanking a vanilla sofa. The coffee table held current issues of *Cosmopolitan* and *TV Guide*, a hammered copper ashtray, and the remote control gizmo for her television set. A small table that may or may not have been a genuine antique had a drawer containing two packs of Bicycle cards and eight woven-cane drink coasters.

There was a picture on the wall, but that probably went with the apartment.

A low cabinet with three doors supported a medium-price

television set, a video cassette recorder, and one of those overly complicated radio-tape players with built-in speakers. It looked like a metal owl.

Under the entertainment gear, inside the cabinet, there was a neat stack of pop and rock tapes and a video of *Jewel of the Nile* that some movie-hire joint would want back one of these days. And a set of good china. And sterling silver, with each knife and fork and spoon tucked into its own sleeve of soft, purple cloth.

I switched off the flashlight and stood in the center of the darkened room, picturing everything I had seen so far. I let my mind go blank and waited for that old Rafferty inspiration to come booming in.

It didn't, so I went back to doing things the hard way.

I went into the bathroom, closed the door, and turned on the light. The tiled cell was apartment bland, though she tried to brighten it up with colorful towels. One of them hung over the sliding glass shower door. A bath mat lay on the floor, rumpled, where she had stood on it to dry herself. A stick-on gadget near the sink held a single toothbrush and a plastic glass. The toothpaste was on the counter. Cricket used the special stuff for people with sensitive teeth, and she rolled the tube up from the bottom as she used it. The tube was almost empty.

Her hair dryer was still plugged in; it lay on the other side of the basin like a futuristic pistol. Near it a brush had several strands of honey-colored hair caught in the bristles.

Outside, the night teetered on the thin edge between Monday and Tuesday, but the bathroom was snap-frozen in a slice of Friday morning. I tried to imagine the atmosphere then, steamy and warm with the smell of freshly bathed woman. I couldn't quite do it, mostly because I kept thinking of how she smelled now.

I snapped off the light and moved on.

Cricket had lived in Dallas long enough to know how cold it can get during a north Texas winter. The hall closet held a heavy coat, a white windbreaker, and a fur stole sheathed in a zipper bag. It might have been mink, rabbit, or anything in between for all I could tell. There was a spare blanket on the top shelf, plus an off-white cowgirl hat and a Monopoly game in an old faded box. There were two cardboard cartons on the floor of the closet, and the one on the left contained the most interesting item I'd found yet.

It was a TV camera; a little one for home video recording, with a rat's nest of cables tucked in with it. A spindly contraption in the closet corner turned out to be a tripod with telescoping legs.

After that it was only a matter of checking the two or three places people hide the sort of thing I expected to find.

There was an unlabeled video in the back of her underwear drawer, under a pile of sheer bikini panties. The tape had been used; the hiding place told me that much.

I took my time working out how to operate her VCR. I didn't want to erase the video by mistake. Finally I found the right button, pushed it, and squatted on the living room floor. The television screen twitched and jerked black bars across a field of white hash.

The first image that came up on the screen was pretty dull. A man sat on Cricket's sofa and talked to someone off camera. At least he moved his mouth and seemed to be talking; there was no audio track on the tape.

The man held his chin up and his eyes wide, the way people do when they want to project their voice but not shout. He was forty-five, give or take a couple of years. He seemed at ease, sitting with one arm flung out along the back of the sofa and his legs crossed at the ankles. He wore a gray suit that didn't bunch up at the back of the neck like mine did. And he had a striped tie and dark shoes.

He was a handsome devil, too, with his graying temples and crisp jawline and take-charge appearance. He looked like an easy seventy-five thousand dollars a year on the corporate hoof.

I worked out where the camera must have been and made a bet with myself about what would happen next.

I won the bet when a woman walked into the screen carrying two drinks. She was tall, good-looking, and she moved with heightened grace; the way women do when they deliberately exhibit themselves. She moved slowly, held her arms out, and tilted her head just so when she handed Executive his drink.

She was either dressed or naked, depending on whether you consider three ounces of lace and nylon to be clothing or decoration.

She sat next to Executive and he half turned to face her, which put his left shoulder and back to the camera. They talked for a few minutes, his face hidden now and her face lowered as she sipped her drink and stroked him with a long series of smoldering up-from-under looks. Then she said something and nodded toward the camera.

Executive jumped. He whirled to face the camera with a panicky look that would have cost him his next stock option if his boss had seen it. He banged his glass down onto the coffee table and came off that sofa like an NFL tackle on the snap.

Executive moved too fast for the inexpensive camera. For a second he was only a blurred rush; then the screen showed the woman laughing, and Executive's butt as he bent over the VCR.

Then the picture went blank.

Almost immediately it came back on. This time the camera was focused on an empty bed. The pillows were in place, but the blanket and top sheet had been stripped away. Nothing at all happened for the twenty seconds it took me to decide the bed on the television screen was the one in the apartment bedroom.

There was no way to tell if the interval between scenes had been minutes, hours, or days. I wondered if the cast of players would be the same for Act Two.

I didn't find out, though, because just then the apartment door opened, the lights came on with a jolt, and a big gun dragged a genial little fat man through the doorway.

CHAPTER SIX

He was short and chubby, and his rumpled suit didn't fit him very well. Except for the gun, he looked like anyone's favorite uncle. He had a broad smile on a round face, almost no hair on his head, and eyebrows like dusty caterpillars. "Pretty shitty lock," he said conversationally.

"Yeah, I thought so, too."

I sat there on the floor, feeling stupid. Way to go, Rafferty, you got caught flat-footed. Flat-butted. Whatever.

Eyebrows said, "You know, old hoss, I think we're gonna get along just fine." He smiled even more widely. It seemed the prospect of our continued friendship pleased him immensely.

"I doubt it," I said. "I hadn't planned to entertain visitors at this hour."

"No, I expect you didn't, at that."

Eyebrows jerked the gun barrel and moved me up and away from the television set just as the picture changed. I caught a glimpse of people on the bed, but I couldn't see who they were.

"Can't stand around here jawing with you all night, hoss," Eyebrows said. "How 'bout you step over into that hallway there? Lean back against one wall and walk your feet wa-a-ay over to the other wall."

31

I did all that, and he smiled. "I thank you. Now, your hands up to the back of your neck . . . fine. That's just fine."

He went to stand in front of the television. The gun watched me continuously. Eyebrows divided his attention between me and the screen. His trained caterpillars jumped once, and he pursed his lips and *tsk-tsk*ed at something on the video. Then he sighed, searched for the stop button, and pushed it.

He ejected the video and shoved it into his suit-coat pocket, then sidestepped to the door. He fumbled behind his back for the knob, opened the door, and backed outside.

"So long, hoss," he said, and he slammed the door. Hard. Loud. His shoes slap-slapped the concrete walkway as he hurried away. About the time I had my feet under me, the fat man banged on a door somewhere and yelled something unintelligible.

I was too slow getting out of Cricket's place. The fat man was long gone. But the uproar he'd made had jangled the nerves of the tense apartment dwellers. I had fleeting unpleasant thoughts about lynch mobs.

I relocked Cricket's door, lost a few more seconds doing so, and wondered whether that was a good idea. Around the courtyard, on both levels, the apartment building was coming alive like a nest of angry hornets. More and more doors popped open. Most of those doors had people coming out through them. A man shouted something hoarse and menacing.

Eyebrows had turned right, so I went left, toward the stairs in the corner away from the street.

My boots clattered on the walkway, which was probably why a lanky man with no shirt stepped out of the end apartment. He had a baseball bat in one hand.

There was just enough light to see his white, toothy grin as he raised the bat to his shoulder, ready to try for the outfield fence with my head.

At the last moment I stepped up the pace and went into him shoulder first. That ruined his swing. I got a brief whiff of stale sweat as I raked the side of my boot sole down his shin and stomped on his instep. He screamed and dropped the bat. I took off again.

There was another hero at the bottom of the stairs, but when I didn't slow down, he backed off, tripped over his own feet, and sat down heavily. I tripped, too, over his outstretched legs, and nearly fell. It took ten long, clumsy strides to run my feet back under my body.

I was halfway down the short side of the courtyard by then, so I kept going, pumping hard for the quiet exit where I had slipped in an hour earlier.

It wasn't quiet now, of course. Loud voices and running feet echoed through the enclosed space. Over the chaos, a woman howled tonelessly, endlessly. I wondered if it was Bev. Then, as I ducked out into the night, someone with brains instead of bravado hit the switches and flooded the courtyard with light.

I ran up the side driveway toward the parking area and the back alley. The shouts and door slams faded behind me as I turned left and jogged down the alley.

A few minutes later, an odd, noisy light came up from behind me. I hopped into a backyard where an overgrown bush drooped over a dilapidated fence. I snuggled against the bush and used it as camouflage while I peered back into the alley.

A big Ford station wagon coasted quietly down the alley with its headlights off and the interior light on. A man in pajamas sat in the front passenger seat and fed fat green shells into an automatic shotgun.

The Ford wagon had just passed me when something fluttered and twitched around my left ankle, then grabbed me firmly.

By the time I realized it was a hand, not a dog or a snake, a bleary but terrifying loud voice mumbled, "Godom getcha fugging seff otta my—"

My first two swings missed. The third clipped him somewhere that hurt us both but shut him up. It was worth a few sore knuckles.

On the other side of the fence, tires scrunched on gravel. The Ford stopped. ". . . heard somepin, damn it," a raspy voice said. "Just listen a minute, will ya?"

Whoever had grabbed me stirred angrily and mumbled

gibberish. I fumbled the blackjack out of my boot, frantically felt for his head and gently flicked the sap against his skull behind the ear. It made a sound like thumping a ripe canta-loupe. He slumped like every bone in his body had melted.

"There!" The voice from the Ford. "Ja hear that?"

Another voice muttered something with a negative tone to it. There was the clunk of an automatic transmission chang-ing gears and the sound of tires rearranging gravel. The big wagon backed up and stopped opposite me.

I was below fence level then, in the shadow of the bush, bent in a runner's starting crouch, with one foot braced against the fence. I had a dim path plotted across the black lawn; a path I hoped would take me around the house and into the next street. I'd make it easily, I decided. Easily.

Unless the shooter had a sidekick with a spotlight.

Approximately twelve years later, the first voice said, "Ain't nothing now. Let's go."

They went. I breathed.

After a quick look up and down the now-dark alley, I used the flashlight, its beam squeezed between two fingers, to see who I had clobbered.

A wino. Or a bum, at least. He looked sixtyish, which meant he could be anything from thirty up. His face was gray and bristly, with dirt caked in the wrinkles. When I felt for a pulse on his neck, a flea jumped onto the back of my hand.

I left the old lush where he lay. He was alive, and the headache he'd have when he woke up would not be a new experience for him. And it was cheaper than Ripple, to boot.

Scuttling along on mental tiptoe, I followed the alley for three more blocks before I cut through a side yard, crossed Gaston Avenue, and strolled toward the Mustang.

I got in, started it, and drove to a shadowed spot a block from the Casa Cahuenga. Then I dug my pipe out of the glove box, fired up, and leaked smoke into the night. And, okay, I trembled a little while I watched the street theater down the block.

A patrol car had pulled up into the Casa Cahuenga's ab-breviated driveway, but the two cops hadn't gotten ten feet

from the car yet. There was quite a crowd telling them what
had happened.

Men waved their arms and postured. "Boy, did that sucker
run when I . . ." Women in bathrobes stood back, hugged
themselves, and shuffled into small groups. "I swear, there
were three of them, Gloria, and one of them had a huge . . ."
The cops nodded and soothed and held long, five-cell flash-
lights in their armpits while they scribbled in pocket note-
books.

I couldn't help remembering how many times I'd answered
that sort of call when I'd carried a badge. It was one of the
reasons I still hated blue serge.

When the cops and the crowd finally went into Casa Cahuenga, I started the Mustang and drove home.

I wheeled down Palm Lane and into my driveway, feeling
dissatisfied. Despite all the hoorah, I was farther behind than
ever. Now I had more questions and still no answers. And I
was coming down from the adrenaline buzz. A muscle in my
back twitched occasionally. My mouth tasted sour.

I left the car in the driveway because it seemed too much
trouble to fight with the balky garage door. I yawned my way
across the front yard with the firm intention of being sound
asleep inside ten minutes.

But the neighborhood Irish setter was out on his rounds.
He barked at me and ran around wanting to play, like he
usually did. Before I could get him shushed up, there were
lights showing in half the houses on the street.

So I finished my day at two-thirty in the morning, sitting
on my front step, with a big, happy, stupid dog chewing on
my pants' cuffs.

CHAPTER SEVEN

The next time I took a look at Tuesday morning, I liked it a whole lot better. At nine-fifteen I was sitting up in bed sipping my first cup of hot black heart-starter and feeling reasonably charitable toward the world and its confusing occupants.

If Hilda had been there, the morning would have been perfect. We might even have burst into song, like Nelson Eddy and Jeanette MacDonald. "I'll be loving you-oo-oo-oo . . . ." I wondered how I'd look in one of those Mountie hats. Pretty good, probably. What the hell, if a bear can wear one . . .

Lounging there, drifting through the wacky morning thoughts, I was hiding from the fact that I had a case that made absolutely no sense. I had expected a simple job; rifle the apartment, read the police file, and tell Winchester the bad news: *So sorry, boss. No file, no loose ends. The cops are right. It was a mugging. Thanks for the fee and bye now.*

But now I had a dead girl who wasn't what she was supposed to be, a video certain to cause trouble for someone, and a fat little bastard I intended to watch eat his own gun.

Thinking about that got me started on the day. I wanted to begin on a pleasant note, so I phoned Hilda at the store and smiled when she said hello to my right ear.

"Hiya, babe, it's me. I'm sorry I didn't make it last night."

"That's okay," she said. "You didn't get into trouble, did you?"

"Hilda! Me?"

"You wouldn't tell me anyway. Look, big guy, I have an absolute bitch of a day going here. Tonight? My place?"

"Definitely. Without fail. Even as we speak, I am compiling a list of the delightful things I intend to do to your ripe and succulent body."

"Yummy. See you then."

"Bye, babe."

On occasion Hilda has wondered how I can have light-hearted, loving conversations with her, then go out into the world and, as she says, "be ugly and severe to people."

Me, I've never found it to be a problem.

The skinny redhead still guarded the entrance to The Green Army. She was making notes in a loose-leaf folder when I stopped in front of her desk. After a moment, she looked up.

"Hi," I said. "Any chance I could see Winchester without getting groped?"

I was trying to keep it light. What the hell, I even smiled to show her I was only kidding.

Her face closed up. "Don't you wish," she said. She slapped her folder shut, stood, and marched off toward Winchester's office door. Halfway there, she turned and said, "Well, come on!"

I caught up with her, and we crossed the rest of the room without speaking. Well, she muttered something once, though I didn't catch exactly what she said.

One thing seemed certain, though. She no longer thought I had "nice buns."

She didn't bother to knock on Winchester's door this time. She opened it, stood aside, and waved me through. The door closed behind me.

Winchester was on the telephone, frowning delicately. He almost cracked his cheeks shifting gears to a broad smile, and he motioned me to the wooden chair opposite him. After a couple of false starts, he cut in on whoever was on the phone and told them he would call back later.

Winchester put the phone down, slapped his hands together, and beamed *bonhomie* across the desk at me. "Well, well, I didn't expect to see you quite so soon."

"Funny you should say that. I didn't expect to be back so soon. But it happens a lot."

"I beg your pardon?"

"Rafferty's Rule Number Seven: Anxious clients who smile too much are usually trouble. You smile too much. So tell me, Winchester, why are you jerking me around?"

Halfway through that broadside, the sunny smile went behind a cloud, and he became very still. He looked at his hands. He didn't say anything.

I stared at him awhile, then went on. "I should have known you were only playing with yourself when you insisted on specific results. Remember what you said? 'Prove Dormac-Chaffee killed Cricket Dawes,' you said, which is a long way from asking me to find out *who* killed Cricket Dawes. And an even longer way from the question I should have asked: who was Cricket Dawes?"

I started filling my pipe and found myself ramming too much tobacco too tightly into the bowl. That didn't matter, though, because I realized if I lighted the pipe in that tiny office, the smoke would drive us out in the first ten seconds.

So I put the pipe away, which stupidly—but naturally—made me even angrier at Winchester.

"I can't believe you actually thought Cricket intended to help you scuttle Dormac-Chaffee. For God's sake, it's so obvious that—" A sudden thought came to me. "Did you ever meet Cricket Dawes? Face to face, I mean?"

"No, I . . ." Winchester's face changed. He jumped up and came around the desk in a hurry, headed for the door. At first I thought he was running away, but he wasn't. He jerked open the office door and bellowed at the front room: "Tom! Linda! Get in here."

Then he stood in the doorway, hands on his hips, and waited. It was like a movie scene; John Wayne summons the young cowpokes who let the rustlers get away. Winchester didn't play it too badly. I wondered if he'd remember to say, "pilgrim."

Tom and Linda tentatively crowded into the tiny office. Tom was a slender youth in an ancient T-shirt with a tropical flower on it. He was trying to grow a mustache, but not doing very well at it.

Linda was the redhead on front-door duty.

Winchester slammed the door and wormed his way past them and behind his desk. It was a struggle to move around with four people in the tiny room. Winchester and I sat in the only chairs. Tom and Linda stood against the longest wall.

The boy Tom shifted his weight from one foot to the other. He darted quick glances from me to Winchester and back again. Linda, on the other hand, seemed mildly amused. At least she was amused when she looked at Winchester. The only time she looked at me, she rolled her eyes and sighed.

Winchester was all squared shoulders and stiff back as he raked the hired help with his eyes. The scowl scared hell out of the boy and bounced off the girl with no visible effect.

Winchester turned to me. "Cricket Dawes phoned us. She asked for me personally. She said she worked at Dormac-Chaffee and wanted to let people know about abnormal radiation levels and other deficiencies at the plant. That was a little more than four weeks ago. I spoke to her for . . . oh, five minutes, perhaps less. After that I relied on my staff." He darted a savage glance at Tom. Tom winced.

"When she first talked to me, Cricket was quite vague," Winchester said. "Frankly, I didn't expect much to come of it. But I turned her over to Tom and instructed him to initiate our standard inside-informant communications channels."

I gave him the look he deserved for mangling the language like that.

He looked back, unrepentant. "People revealing inside information about their employers are at risk. They cannot afford to be seen or overheard here. So we protect them. The staff member responsible for liaison uses their home phone or phone booths to contact the informant. All hard evidence is transferred by mail or by prearranged meetings in crowded public places. It is a very effective system."

"Oh, I'm sure it is." I waved my hand at Tom. "So you handed Cricket off to Secret Agent X-14 here. Then what?"

Winchester refused to be baited. "Tom gave Cricket a standard briefing sheet for corporate informers, a nuclear-industry questionnaire, and a memo explaining our contact procedure."

"That must have been pretty exciting for Tom. Did the girl here do anything useful?"

The amusement dropped out of her eyes like changing TV channels. She snapped at me in a cold voice. "I am not *the girl*! You can call me Linda or Ms. Taree or Hey You, but don't you call me the goddamn *girl*!"

"Okay," I said, "that's a fair point. I intended to insult you, but not on the grounds of gender. I apologize, Ms. Taree."

She nodded fiercely and stared at the wall above my head.

I said, "Now it's your turn."

"My turn? What the hell are you talking about?"

"Your turn to apologize," I said. "Yesterday you clutched me to win a twenty-dollar office bet. That was *très* droll and liberated, no doubt. But what if *I* had clutched *you* to win a bet? Would that have been droll? No way, and you know it. Accordingly, I am owed an apology." I shook my head sadly. "It was quite a slur. Genderwise."

Linda Taree stared at me for a long time.

I said, "I'm also miffed because you didn't offer to split the twenty with me."

She dropped her head and shook it back and forth. "I give up," she said. "I could try to explain about affirmative action and positive discrimination but I think . . ." She looked up. Something I couldn't identify glinted in her eyes. "I accept your apology, Mr. Rafferty. And I also apologize." She extended her right arm and we shook hands. We grinned at each other.

About then, I realized Winchester and Tom were staring at us with big eyes and wondering looks on their faces.

"What's the matter with you guys?" I said. "Didn't you think I could get along with modern women?"

CHAPTER EIGHT

Linda Taree's rueful grin seemed to say word-for-word what I was thinking: We can get along, I suppose, but you sure do get carried away at times.

I couldn't tell what Winchester was thinking; his expression had changed from dumbfounded to calculating. Tom? He simply looked nervous.

We all waited like that for a few moments, like a posh cocktail party frozen in the split second after a drunk collapsed. Eventually Winchester cleared his throat and continued as if nothing had happened. "Linda was the alternate contact for Cricket. Tom and Linda worked the file together."

"Who was in charge?"

Winchester threw a glance at Linda before he answered me. "Neither of them. As I said, they worked the file together. We don't have bosses here."

"Except you."

Nobody wanted to look at that idea for very long.

"Tell me something," I said. "Have any of you ever been to Cricket's apartment?"

Head shakes all around.

"Did any of you ever spend more than a few moments with her; ever talk to her to find out why she wanted to hurt her employer; ever check her out to make sure she was who she said she was?''

More head shakes, slower and more thoughtful this time.

"Okay," I said, "I think I see how this screwup happened. Send them out, Winchester. We need to talk."

"Dammit, Rafferty, you can't treat people like that."

"I work for people, not committees." I had to tell Winchester I'd burgled Cricket's apartment. I wasn't ready to do that in front of second-string personnel. "Make up your mind," I said to Winchester. "Do you want to hear the rest of it or not?"

I sat and stared at Winchester, wondering if he had the guts to kick me out.

He didn't; he wriggled out from behind his desk and shepherded Linda and Tom out of the office. There were angry whispers, patted shoulders, and finally, the clack of the latch.

I waited until he ran the obstacle course again and slumped into his chair; then I opened my wallet and counted out his six hundred dollars. I removed two fifties from the stack and returned them to my wallet.

"That's a half day's pay for last night and this little chat. You have about ten minutes still on the meter. After that you have to decide whether I keep working or go away and leave you to your pipe dreams."

Winchester picked up the money and riffled through it. He put the stack down exactly in the center of his desk and said, "Go on. Tell me this mysterious 'rest of it.' ''

"Okay. Point one: you're getting carried away. Parlaying Cricket's phone call into imaginary hired killers in company ties is soap opera stuff."

"Every company in the nuclear industry has blood on its hands, Rafferty."

"I wouldn't know. A guy I talked to seems to agree with you, but that doesn't mean it's true. Anyway, we're not talking about atomic whizbangs here; we're talking about people. I know about people, and I'm telling you there was no reason for Dormac-Chaffee to kill Cricket Dawes."

Winchester looked exasperated. "The files, Rafferty! She was about to expose them."

"What files? We don't even know they exist. And if they do, Cricket wouldn't have gotten away with them. Any middle manager worth his office carpet could have fired Cricket, stood over her while she cleaned out her desk, then marched her off the property. Good-bye, problem."

"But what if she already had the files?" Winchester said. "That's different, isn't it?"

"Not much. Let's say Cricket lifted the files earlier and hid them. In that case, the Vice President in Charge of Firing Uppity Secretaries would fire Cricket and threaten her with no final paycheck, a police investigation, and being blacklisted at every company and employment agency in town. If her job involved a government security clearance, he'd mutter about the FBI and treason and motherhood and apple pie.

"But," I went on, "let's say Cricket was a real martyr-rebel prepared to suffer any indignity to save the world from the fascist polluting swine."

I showed Winchester my big round innocent eyes. "Am I getting the slogans right?"

His lips were thin and pale. "You're telling this fairy tale. Get on with it."

"Oh, right. Well, while Cricket played resistance-leader-in-the-Gestapo-dungeon, Dormac-Chaffee security men would search for the files. They would go through her desk first, then a personal locker, if the employees have lockers. Next thing, they'd toss her car. If they didn't find anything right off, they'd drive the car away and strip it down to spare parts. Later on they could claim it was stolen from the parking lot. And other security guys—or maybe a free-lancer—would break into her apartment."

"But all that takes time," Winchester said. "They couldn't hold her indefinitely."

"Long enough. They might try to stall her, or they might just close the gates. A facility like that must have some way to isolate itself; some alert procedure, like a military base."

"Umm, you might be right."

"Count on it. The point is, they would find the files. And they wouldn't have to lay a hand on her."

"Very well. Suppose you're right about that part. But as

long as she could talk about the files, she would be a threat to them. Wouldn't they want to silence her?''

"They could do that without killing her." I shook my head and wiggled around trying to find a soft spot in the wooden chair. Explaining the facts of life to a grown man was hard work.

"Big companies know how to put out the sort of brushfire you want to start. Imagine the lunchtime conversations at golf clubs and expense account restaurants. Executives stroking publishers. Lawyers mumbling about libel and slander. Hell, they could probably trot in a tame general to harrumph about national security. And television stations would get phone calls from Washington about public responsibility, with a reminder of when their license comes up for renewal. If the story got published at all, it would be in a supermarket scandal sheet nobody believes anyway. Face it, Winchester, ants can't stop lawn mowers.''

He frowned. "I just don't understand you. The way you talk, you should be on our side, but—''

"But you're as bad as they are. You assemble a bunch of envelope stuffers and think you're freeing the downtrodden masses from the yoke of the exploitive developers and rapists of the environment. Or whatever the current emotive phrase happens to be.''

I wanted a pipe, and I couldn't smoke in that stuffy little office, which made me irritated, and it was easy to blame Winchester for that.

"And you're paranoid as hell,'' I said. "Imagining bugs on the phones and inventing buzzword gimmicks like 'informant communications channels,' for God's sake. Well, you shot yourself in the foot this time. You were all busy playing secret agent, and nobody bothered to look at Cricket Dawes to see who or what she was.''

"You are incredibly cynical. Why can't you accept that Cricket simply cared about the environment?''

"Let me tell you about Cricket Dawes. Last night I got into her apartment. Cricket Dawes ate white bread and red meat and sugary breakfast cereal and whipped margarine. She bought imported vodka and probably drank wine only on special occasions. She smoked cigarettes. She had a fur and good silver. Her apartment was so neat and orderly, she may have been a compulsive cleaner.''

He looked blank. I went on. ''Cricket Dawes was no environmentalist, at least not the way you people are. Cricket was not a vegetarian. She did not eat brown bread or granola or wheat germ or bean sprouts. That was the key, Winchester. What she *didn't* have in her apartment. There was no jug of rough red wine. No roach holders. No posters of baby seals, no slogans, no macrame wall decorations. No plants, only cut flowers. No antiestablishment literature. No books at all, in fact, let alone alternative life-style softcovers printed on recycled paper. Cricket tended toward glossies with quizzes to tell her if she was having properly sophisticated orgasms.''

Winchester started to interrupt. I patted the air between us to forestall his complaint.

''All right, all right, I know those are clichés. I know there's no such thing as a typical environmentalist with all those characteristics. But Cricket didn't have any of those traits. Not a single one. From all the evidence, she was exactly the opposite.''

Winchester looked pained. ''Well . . .''

''Trust me on this one,'' I said. ''You misread Cricket Dawes. As far as I can tell, she was just another working gal who screwed the wheels off the boss whenever he could get away from his wife.''

''How do you know that?''

''Cricket tried to make a home porno movie one night, but her boyfriend didn't think much of the idea.''

''Are you certain he was her boss?''

''Not entirely. He's somebody's boss, though, and people usually screw around in their own offices.''

''How do you know he's married?''

''He's twenty years older than she was, for one thing. He was lolling around on her sofa in his office clothes while she mixed drinks in a seduction costume. He doesn't keep a razor or toothbrush in her apartment. And when he realized the candid camera was running, he panicked and turned it off. Take it as gospel: he's married.''

"You mean the tape didn't show . . ."

"Well, later on there was a bed. Empty at first, then with people on it, but I'm not sure it was them. I was interrupted. A little fat guy smiled his way in, and he got away with the video."

Winchester loved that part. Big grin, lots of teeth and crinkly laugh lines. "You let someone take the video away from you?"

"He was only a little guy, but he had a fair-sized gun."

Winchester spread his hands wide. "Well, there you are, then. Dormac-Chaffee, after the files."

"No. He didn't search for anything. I had already found the video, and that was all he wanted."

Winchester smirked. "Perhaps. Perhaps. Well, at least now I know where you're coming from. You're being hard-nosed and macho because you're embarrassed. You lost your big clue. Your pride is bent."

"I admit I feel stupid about that. Hell, I'll help you heap ashes on me. I was a bad boy. I screwed up. Woe is me." I looked at him. "Do you have any more abuse you'd like to get out on the table?"

Winchester grinned; one of those boy-next-door grins Norman Rockwell painted. "No," he said, "not right now."

"Okay. Then let's get down to the nut-cutting. Cricket's purse seems to be missing, which points to a robbery. This probably did not start as a murder. Maybe she fought or screamed and the guy flipped out. These things happen. The second possibility is a hassle involving the boyfriend and, maybe, the video. And running a poor third is Dormac-Chaffee. A very poor third."

"Well, that's your opinion." Winchester scrunched his eyebrows together thoughtfully. "If I keep you on the job, what will you do now?"

I shook my head. "No, not that way. Don't try to turn this around and interview me about how I work. The only thing I will do is find out who killed her. If I can. And quite possibly, I can't. Meantime you're a client, not a supervisor. Oh, and no more bullshit about forcing the facts to implicate

Dormac-Chaffee, either.'' I leaned back in the chair and waited to get fired.

"You are an egotistical, offensive son of a bitch, Rafferty.'' He said it conversationally, as if commenting about the weather.

"Mother loved me.''

"Hmm. She was doubtless the last person to do so.'' He picked up the stack of money, bounced it against an open palm, then put it down on the edge of the desk near my elbow. "Stick with it,'' he said. "I'm willing to gamble, mainly because I still believe you're wrong. Dormac-Chaffee *is* behind Cricket's death.''

I did not pick up the cash. "You are absolutely certain you want me to continue?''

"I'm certain. Because I think you are pigheaded enough to find out the truth and because I think I know what the truth is. However, there is one thing. You are an employee of The Green Army, and you should show respect for our goals and—''

He stopped when the money hit him on the chest. "Wait, goddamn it!'' He came up out of his chair and followed me to the door. He pushed the now-ragged wad of bills at me and said, "All right, all right. Take it. Take it and go!''

After ten seconds or so, I took the money. As soon as I touched it, Winchester let go, like it burned his fingers. He chewed his lower lip while I straightened the bills and put them into my wallet. He started to sit down, changed his mind, opened his mouth, closed his mouth, and finally he perched on the corner of his desk and stared at me.

I left, then turned and leaned back into his office doorway. I smiled and waggled my fingers at him.

"Bye, boss.''

CHAPTER NINE

I took Hilda to lunch at a new barbecue place not far from my office. I should have taken her someplace closer to her office.

"Hey, big guy," she said, "remember way back ten minutes ago, when you assured me no one could make a greasy egg salad sandwich?"

I nodded because I couldn't talk. I was doing unspeakable things to a sparerib at the time.

"You were wrong," Hilda said.

Actually, the ribs weren't very good, either. We decided the new barbecue place would never survive to become an old barbecue place, gave up on the food, and lunched on Lowenbrau. At least the beer wasn't greasy.

After a longish quiet spell, Hilda said, "Tell me, sonny. Were you watching from the curb when that nasty old truck ran over your puppy dog?"

"That bad, huh?"

"Well, if I hadn't seen that expression on your face before, I'd be worried."

"Sorry, babe. This stupid Dawes case bugs me."

Hilda sipped beer, then said, "The Dawes case. That's the one that's going to mess up our plans for a weekend in San Antonio, right?"

"Wrong! Off to old San Antone on Friday. Absolutely. I've

already packed my Davy Crockett cap, so I can wear it to the Alamo.''

She sighed and smiled. ''Sure you have. Look, we could wait until after my St. Louis buying trip. If you need more time for this, uh, Dawes thing.''

''Naw, it's a simple case, really. Full of weird people, though. Well, maybe not weird, but people I don't like much.'' I told her about Winchester, Linda the redhead, Dormac-Chaffee, and the little fat man who took away the video.

Hilda's eyes didn't like the part about the fat man and his gun, but she didn't say anything.

''And there's another thing,'' I said. ''My client hasn't bothered to say he's sorry that the Dawes woman is dead. I don't expect weeping and wailing and gnashing of teeth; a simple, 'Damn, what a shame,' would do. But Winchester just smiles boyishly and fantasizes about headlines.''

''While his secretary gropes the nether regions I know and love,'' Hilda said. ''I hope that sort of thing doesn't happen often.''

''Being a male sex symbol is a terrible burden,'' I said. ''You have no idea.''

''Right.''

I finished my beer and sighed. ''Do you seriously think I like being accosted on the street by hordes of women? But, never fear, I shall remain faithful.''

''You do that.''

''Tell you what,'' I said, ''you know the big horsehide sofa in your office?''

Hilda squinted and nodded. ''I have a buyer for that piece, I think.''

''Let 'em wait. Let's go hit the old sofa, babe. I'll jump on your bones. How's that for fidelity?''

''And to think my friends say you have no class.''

Despite the fun word games, Hilda and I went back to work after lunch. I dropped her at the store in time for her one-thirty appointment with a Houston oil man. Hilda said the oillionaire had more money than sense, which seemed a reasonable conclusion to me. The guy had made a special trip to Dallas to dicker on a gateleg ivory-handled Edwardian snuffbox or some damn thing.

Me, I went to check in with the cops. I really didn't know much about Cricket's death, despite the fancy theories I had used to beat Winchester about the head and shoulders. Now, belatedly, it was time to run down the facts.

Besides, the quest for knowledge is always a worthwhile goal. And you can quote me on that.

CHAPTER TEN

I found Lieutenant Ed Durkee drinking coffee from a mug with his name on it and arguing baseball with a uniformed patrolman. Both men leaned against a wall in an upstairs corridor at the Dallas cop shop.

You have seen that corridor. Everyone who has watched television since 1963 has seen that corridor. When you saw it on the tube, Ed Durkee's predecessors had a man named Oswald in handcuffs. They walked him down the corridor. There were a lot of shouting reporters in the background. A few days later Oswald was dead, and the cops had Jack Ruby. Same cuffs, same walk, same reporters. Everyone knows that corridor.

Ed Durkee was a big man; a sloppy bear of a man with droopy jowls and a pear-shaped body. He wore a rumpled brown suit every day of his working life.

Durkee drained his coffee mug, swung his big sad face toward me and grunted, "You. Thought I'd have to send Ricco out after you."

The uniformed cop watched us both.

"What is this?" I said. "Here I am, a public-spirited citizen seeking conversation and solace from the defenders of Big D, and I have to put up with verbal abuse. Wait until the ACLU hears about this."

"Smart ass," Durkee said. He heaved himself away from

the wall and hitched up his trousers. "Come on, Rafferty. I wanna talk to you." Ed shambled off without looking back to see if I was following him.

The patrolman looked at me. He had a half smile on his face.

"Officer," I said, "I believe I'm about to encounter police brutality. You can be a witness for me, if you like."

The cop laughed and walked away. I followed Ed.

I caught him at the coffee machine. Ed refilled his mug, I swiped the cleanest one I could find, and we stood there sipping bitter black coffee and wondering what the other one was up to. At least, that's what I was wondering.

"What the hell do you want, Rafferty?" Aha, that's what Ed was wondering, too.

"Thought we might compare notes on this Cricket Dawes thing."

"Cricket what? Oh, that mugging on Gaston Avenue. What's your interest?"

I said, "I have a client who thinks it wasn't a mugging. He thinks Dawes was killed by the people she worked for."

Ed said, "You believe that?"

"No. And I told the client he was wrong, but it's his money."

"This client. He anybody I should know about?"

I shook my head. "No one with a reason to hurt her. He's worried about what happened to her."

"You been out to the girl's apartment?" Ed idly examined his coffee cup. He was about as subtle as an elephant in an aloha shirt.

"Yeah. I talked to her neighbors last night."

"Funny thing, how they all seemed to think you had some strange name that didn't sound a bit like Rafferty."

"Hell, Ed, you know how people are. They don't listen. They get names mixed up. In fact, I've often worried about the deleterious effect that confused eyewitness reports have on diligent police work."

"I'll bet you have." He took a noisy slurp of his coffee. "You find anything interesting in her apartment?"

"I wasn't in her apartment. I only talked to a few people

around the pool and then left.'' I trotted out a puzzled look and showed it to him. "Ed, where are you going with this?"

He gave me thirty seconds to break down and babble the truth at him. Stout fellow that I am, I resisted. Eventually he said, "How you can stand there with that goofy look on your face. . . ."

"Wouldn't have the faintest idea what you're talking about, Ed."

"Uh-huh. We had a prowler-call out there last night."

"That doesn't surprise me. Those folks are pretty goosey. Some dog probably knocked over a garbage can."

"Not quite. Couple of eyewits say they saw a man come out of the girl's apartment. And one guy swears up and down a great big dude beat the shit out of him with a baseball bat. Sure that wasn't you?"

"Well, it is true that I'm a fine example of manhood, but I don't know about 'great big dude.' Oh, and I'm not carrying a concealed Louisville slugger. You want to frisk me?"

"Shut up, Rafferty," Ed said in a bored tone.

"Might have been a burglary. Somebody working off the obit columns."

"Haw! The squad report says no evidence of burglary. And the door was locked. The manager had to let the patrol guys in."

"Ed, come on! Who ever heard of a burglar locking the door behind him? That was not a righteous complaint."

"Maybe. You still got a set of lockpicks?"

"I am shocked," I said. "Lockpicks are burglary tools. Why, a man could get arrested for carrying things like that."

"Yeah."

"Ed, if you're finished with this humbug, why don't we sit down somewhere and trade information?"

"You got anything for me?"

"A little, maybe. Not much."

Ed shrugged and said, "Why not? Go wait in my office; I'll get Ricco to sit in."

Ed was pawing through his overloaded in-basket when Ricco bopped into the office. Ricco walked oddly; he affected a choppy arrhythmic stride he thought was hip and street-smart. Which went with the rest of Ricco. He was short, skinny, and super neat in loud sport jackets and even louder leisure suits. Imagine Nathan Detroit on a starvation diet.

Ricco wan't a bad cop, actually; it was just awfully hard to take him seriously.

"Hey, Rafferty," Ricco said, "blow away any bad guys this week?"

"Been pretty quiet lately, Ricco."

"Don't worry," he said, "things'll pick up."

Ed said, "If you two can stop trying to out-Rambo each other, could we maybe get some work done?"

"Okay," I said, "first, do either of you get any environmentalist vibrations from this Dawes woman? Could she be an antinuclear nut? Or anything at all in that line?"

"Naw," Ricco sneered, "just another gash, as far as I can see. Ah, her clothes might be a little fancy for her salary, but not enough to think she was hooking or dealing."

"Okay. That fits with what I hear, too. My client disagrees, though. He thinks she was an outraged conservationist about to blow the whistle on Dormac-Chaffee."

Ricco said, "Naw. Not this chickie."

Ed Durkee rumbled, "I'm not impressed so far, Rafferty. Your client's wet dreams don't count as information."

"True. Try this. I hear she was having it off with a handsome corporate type. Might have been her boss, but I don't know for sure."

Ed had found the Dawes file. He opened it. "What's the stud's name? According to this, she worked as a secretary or assistant or something to a guy named Walter Hadley."

"I don't have a name. He's maybe forty-five, dark hair, graying temples. Sharp but conservative dresser. Executive type."

Durkee looked at me wearily. "That's all you have on him?"

"I've never seen him. I only got a partial description here and there. You know how it is."

"Hell I do. You're holding out something, Rafferty. What kind of a description doesn't have height and weight in it?"

"You know what eyewitnesses always say, Ed. Medium. He was medium height, medium weight."

Ed scowled at me, but Ricco grinned and ruined the effect. Finally Ed said, "Okay, okay. So what's with this guy? Were they shacking up?"

"No, I don't think so. Probably just a quickie now and then. How about you take a turn now?"

"Oh, hell," Ed said, "we don't have much, either." He flipped back and forth through the file. "Sandra Dawes, female Cauc, twenty-six years old, her address you know. Her job you know. Lemme see here, found beside her car—a white 1983 Toyota Corolla, if it matters—behind her apartment building. Call logged at five-o-seven on Friday the ninth. Preliminary medical says no sexual assault. Purse missing. Facial wounds. No eyewits. It looks like a mugging that went wrong. It is funny one way, though."

"Funny how, Ed?"

He looked up, and his basset hound face seemed droopier than normal. "Funny odd, not funny ha-ha. See, she wasn't killed in a normal way. Hell, she wasn't really *killed*. It was more like an accident."

Ricco sniffed at the sloppy sentimentalism. I waited for Ed to go on.

"I don't have a full PM report yet, only these notes Ricco made after he talked to the medical examiner." Ed searched for, and found, a piece of paper in the file. "Okay, here's the story. Somebody popped her one in the mouth. Loosened a couple of teeth; cut up the inside of her mouth; split her lower lip; bruised the upper lip. And gave her a nosebleed. A pretty bad nosebleed."

Ricco took over. "I figure it went down like this. Mugger—who could be any of a couple of hundred assholes around town—is diddly-bopping down that alley looking for whatever trouble he can get into. He sees the Dawes fox pull in and park. She gets out of her car. Mugger eases over and feeds her a knuckle sandwich; then he grabs her purse and runs. Well, hey, five seconds later he's only a cloud of dust two blocks down the alley, right? Meantime, this Dawes cookie, she'd falling down, which ain't hard to understand, since this scumbag's been pounding on her face. But when she falls down, she lands on her back and bangs her head on the concrete." Ricco shrugged broadly. "Lights out, baby."

I said, "Ed, what is he saying? The bump on her head was the cause of death?"

"No," Ed said, "that's what I was telling you. The bump only knocked her out. The nosebleed killed her. She drowned."

"Oh, Christ, Ed."

"Yeah. Crazy, isn't it? Every goddamn Saturday night two dozen guys get their faces busted up worse than that, fighting in cowboy bars just for the fun of it. But this woman, Dawes, just happened to land on her back and knock herself out for a few minutes. Her lungs filled up with blood, the ME says."

None of us spoke for a while. Finally, Ricco said, "That's all we got, Rafferty. And it's all we're likely to ever get, unless we grab some asshole for another mugging and he cops to this one. And I will give attractive odds we don't never get that lucky."

"Yeah," I said. "Look, there is one other thing. My client thinks Dawes may have stolen certain files from her office at Dormac-Chaffee. Was there anything like that in her car?"

Ed looked at Ricco, who shook his head. "No files in the apartment, either," Ed said, "though I suspect you already know that."

"Have you interviewed the people she worked with?"

"Not yet," Ricco said. "I'm gonna, but it was low on the list, seeing as how she was wasted at home, not work. But this business about her screwing the boss is kinda interesting."

Ed stabbed a pudgy figure at me. "And if you get anything more, I expect to see you in a big hurry."

"Sure."

"But, you know," Ricco said, "this don't feel right as a lover's quarrel. If this dude is a fancy business type, it don't figure he'd be slapping her around in a parking lot. Guys like that are too uptight about their images. In her apartment or a no-tell motel, sure, but not in a parking lot." Ricco shook his head. "I'll check it out, but I still like the mugging angle."

Durkee said, "All right, Rafferty, get lost. We got work to do."

"In a minute. Do you have a picture of her?"

"This one from the morgue, that's all." It was a four by six flash picture clipped inside the file folder. Ed pulled it loose and slid it across his desk to me.

They had cleaned her up for the photo, but it didn't help much. If anything, it made the damage more obvious. Her mouth was swollen and torn. Her eyes were open, but her lids drooped and gave her a dull, slightly stupid, look. Her teeth were stained with dried blood. Her hair was tangled.

She had been much prettier on the video.

Poor dead Cricket.

That's the way I found myself thinking of her as I looked at the picture. There were so many ways she might have died. Freeway accident, apartment house fire, cancer, even old age.

But Cricket Dawes beat all the odds because she happened to land on her back after a punch that should have left her with only a fat lip and a grudge.

Drowned in her own blood. In a crummy parking lot. Poor dead Cricket.

"Holy shit, Rafferty," Ricco said, "you're mooning over that goddamn picture like she was your long lost girlfriend."

I handed the photo back to Ed. "No. The funny thing is, I don't think I would have liked her at all," I said. "When she was alive."

Out on the street a few minutes later, I decided I needed cheering up. The usual remedy for the Rafferty megrims involves Hilda and conversation and just being together. A severe case calls for a little necking, maybe.

But it was too early to pick up Hilda, so I had to devise other curatives.

There was an insurance case that had been dragging on

and on. It would be nice to clean that up before the weekend and the San Antonio trip.

And surely, if I could catch Willy Barchek, I would be restored to my normal happy self. I decided to give it a shot.

CHAPTER ELEVEN

Willy Barchek was a salesman for an aluminum-pipe factory. Or, at least, he had been a salesman until three months earlier when he'd tripped over a pipe offcut somebody left in the wrong place. Willy said he had twisted his back and crippled himself. Maybe he really had. And maybe not. The insurance company who wrote the workman's comp policy didn't think so.

The insurers had good reasons to be suspicious. Willy's doctor was a quack named Boyle; they called him Bad-Back Boyle on the courthouse steps. Boyle spent so much time testifying for insurance claimants he barely found time to practice medicine. It was a profitable career, though, to judge from Bad-Back's Highland Park home and Mercedes. Maybe the jealousy factor was part of the reason why Bad-Back's name on a medical report was a red rag to the insurance bulls.

The other problem with Willy Barchek's credibility was his lawyer; a shyster so scummy he gave ambulance chasing a bad name.

Of course, all this didn't mean Willy wasn't really hurt. His choice of doctor and lawyer didn't prove he was a fraud. But the insurance company thought he was, and I thought he *probably* was, and catching him would be a small victory to lift the flagging spirits on a day like this, and that's why I headed north and east from downtown.

Willy Barchek lived in a crowded clutch of town houses near Swiss Avenue. He had a Bronco parked at the curb. The Bronco was big and bright red and tall enough to roller-skate under. It had winches and giant black tubular bumpers and gas-can racks and a CB antenna, and it looked like it could drive up the side of Reunion Tower. It was just the sort of vehicle Willy needed to navigate the trackless wastes between his town house and the bowling alley.

I parked where I could see the Bronco but not the Barchek front door and windows, which meant they couldn't see me. Then I went for a stroll. While I walked, I flipped a coin and whistled.

Damned if I didn't drop that coin in front of Barchek's place. And it skittered off the curb right by the Bronco's front tire, would you believe? And you know how hard coins are to pick up, so it was five or ten seconds before I continued my stroll.

Willy Barchek's tire went flat around the same time, but I wouldn't know anything about that.

Then I went back to the Mustang, climbed behind the wheel, got the camera ready, and waited.

In my line of work, you do a lot of sitting around waiting for something to happen. The way to avoid going crazy is to entertain yourself. Virtuous pastimes are good; lofty intellectual thoughts, listening to classical music, taped educational courses, things like that. On the other hand, vices work just as well. I dug out my pipe and tobacco pouch.

Hilda says smoking a pipe is the ultimate displacement activity. She's probably right. By the time you organize the paraphernalia, then do all that blowing and packing and lighting and puffing and tamping, you've nearly forgotten why you wanted a smoke in the first place.

I got it lit, eventually, and huffed blue smoke out the window. It was a still day and the smoke hung around the Mustang. I hoped Willy didn't have conscientious neighbors; one of them might phone me in as a car fire.

While I waited for Willy to do something nice for my side,

I thought about the Winchester–Green Army–Cricket Dawes job. So far, the main problem was that I couldn't sort out all the players.

Cricket Dawes, for example. Everything I'd seen pointed away from environmentalism. Hell, Cricket would have become a yuppie at the drop of an American Express gold card. So why did she approach The Green Army with an outraged-citizen story?

Winchester? A hotshot conservationist with tunnel vision. I guessed his version of events was true as far as he saw them; his mistake about Cricket had been sloppy, not untruthful, but he'd bear watching because he could talk himself into almost anything. And I still didn't like the way he sloughed off Cricket's death as a tiny misstep on the glorious road to environmental nirvana.

The redhead, Linda Taree. She had nearly bitten my head off because I carelessly referred to her as a "girl," then she backed off almost immediately. Well, okay, anyone can over-react momentarily, but thinking back, it hadn't been quite like that. And I didn't think she had suddenly fallen sway to my powerful logic and oratory.

There was Cricket's boss, too. Walter Hadley, Ed had called him. I bet myself a steak dinner against no beer for a week that Hadley would turn out to be the boardroom bandito from Cricket's video.

And then there was the player who confused me the most; the one I'd tucked away to mentally ripen. Who the hell was the little fat guy who got away with that video? Where did he fit in? And how long would it take me to—

Then Willy Barchek's wife came home from her day shift at Dallas Medical and Surgical. She gave the lopsided Bronco a funny look and pulled her yellow Pinto into the garage.

About two minutes later, Willy stormed out to the curb. He stood by the Bronco and glared at the world.

Then Willy changed the tire.

Willy was terrific. I got two pictures of him hauling the spare tire out of the Bronco, four snaps of vigorous jack-handle pumping, and a beautiful sequence when he jerked the flat tire loose and threw it halfway across the street.

As I drove away, I figured it cost Willy Barchek at least one hundred and fifty thousand dollars to change that tire.

CHAPTER TWELVE

"You'd better go through that one more time," Hilda said. "I don't see how you can prove a mugger killed that woman without catching the mugger."

"Elementary, my dear sweet buns, all I have to—"

"*Sweet buns?*"

"It seems appropriate."

The big bed was rumpled and still too warm for any covers. Hilda lay on her stomach but had raised up on her elbows, which created the most perfect flowing line of all time; a line from her raised shoulder down her back past that mole, then up with the swell of her hip and . . . well, the point is, "sweet buns" was exactly the word.

"But," I said, "if you object to 'sweet buns' on moral or sexist grounds, I will—"

"Mostly I object because it sounds like a pickup line in a cowboy bar." Hilda elbow-walked to the edge of the bed, reached over, and came up with her wine glass.

I made a *tsk-tsk* noise and said, "Getting picked up in cowboy bars, my, my. It's a good thing we met and I've taken you away from all that, babe."

She poked me in the side and nearly spilled her wine. "Ho, ho, big guy. Go on, tell me how you're going to do this fancy sleuthing."

I scowled at her fiercely. I probably didn't do a very good

job of it, though, because scowling fiercely is not something I do well when I'm flat on my back, naked, balancing a beer glass on my stomach. We all have our little inadequacies.

"As I was saying when I was rudely interrupted, it's elementary, babe. Old Sherlock was right. Eliminate the impossible, and whatever's left, no matter how improbable, is the answer. Now let's see what we can eliminate. We can safely rule out suicide and Vegan death rays, I think. I'll have to check out her family and background, but let's assume I don't turn up any ex-boyfriends with police records. That leaves only three possibilities: mugger, executive boyfriend, and Dormac-Chaffee. I can prove that one of them did it by eliminating the others. Simple."

"Doesn't sound so simple to me," Hilda said. She had returned to that position again, except she had bent her left knee now. She idly waggled her leg. Idle leg-waggling did nice things to that wonderful line.

"Well," I said, "we're not talking about legal proof. All I have to do is come up with enough common sense data to keep my client happy."

Hilda's leg stopped moving, and she carefully examined the wine in her glass. "And what about the man who took the video?"

"Him. Well, okay. I want to find him, but with no place to start looking, I don't see what I can do."

Hilda said very quietly, "Bull. You're hoping that while you're running around chasing the others, you'll frighten the fat man out in the open." She looked up and locked eyes with me. "You call that 'beating the bushes,' and you've done it before."

A long few moments later, I said, "Hey, just think how much fun we're going to have in San Antonio. Picture this: dinner under the stars beside the river, then a leisurely stroll down the Paseo del Rio, and finally back to the hotel, where moonlight, tender murmurs, and gentle caresses culminate in mad, passionate love on the balcony."

Hilda rubbed her nose and smiled. "Sounds fun but slightly public."

"Hey, no sweat. Every time I sell a ticket, I'll tell them to hold their applause until the end."

"You're crazy, you know that?"

"Maybe not. Have you considered that I might be the normal one and the rest of you are, well, just a little—"

She tried to tickle me then, which was silly, since she's a lot more ticklish than I am. It was fun, though, and after we'd gotten all that out of our systems we settled down in each other's arms, nuzzling like drowsy kittens.

About ten minutes later Hilda said sleepily, "Tell me what you're thinking." When she spoke, her lips brushed my neck. It felt nice.

"I'm thinking about tomorrow. I've decided to start with Walter Hadley."

"Workaholic," she said blearily. "Witchun's Waller Haley?"

I told her and tried to guess aloud what he'd be like. I assumed Hadley was the executive boyfriend, and I invented a big house for him. The family car would be a Volvo station wagon with a Labrador in the back, but Walter would drive a company car; an Olds, maybe. I fell asleep before I got much farther than that.

I was awake early, when the windows were only faintly gray. Hilda's breath was slow and deep. It made a nice, comfortable sound.

After a while I decided I wasn't going back to sleep, so I eased out of bed and got the phone book. There was only one Walter Hadley listed, and the address looked promising, so I dressed, left Hilda a note, and went to see how well I'd guessed.

The house was big, and the company car was a blue Olds. There was an Audi beside it in the garage, though, not a Volvo. And when Hadley's wife waved good-bye from the door, a gangly red setter escaped, not a Labrador. Still, two out of four ain't bad.

Hedley dropped his garage door by remote control and pulled out of the drive without looking back at his wife. I followed him.

Three blocks later, still in deepest suburbia, the street ran through a park as it crossed a small creek. The park was small, too; the size of three basketball courts, say, with a dozen thin trees. It seemed a suitable spot for a kidnapping.

I pulled the Mustang up beside Hadley, pointed frantically at his front wheel and yelled a string of excited nonsense. He stopped. So did I. By the time I'd walked back to him, he was standing by the front of the Olds with a puzzled look on his sculptured face.

"It was that wheel," I said. "Damn thing was going around and around."

He looked at it before he really heard what I'd said. "But—"

I lifted my loose shirttail to let him see the hip-holstered .38. "Let's talk," I said.

Hadley jerked back against the fender and froze. He was pale. His right hand trembled and drummed softly against the shiny blue metal.

"Relax, for Christ's sake," I said. "I'm not going to shoot you. I just wanted to get your attention."

"Who are you?" Some of the shock was flowing away now, with something else replacing it. Suspicion?

"Just another fan," I said. "I caught your latest film. I especially enjoyed the sensitive interpretation of random pro-creative activity underscored by the seamy background of marital infidelity."

"Whaa—"

"Pay attention, will you? The video of you playing hide-the-salami with Cricket Dawes."

Hadley's face lost some of the suspicion and topped up with anger. "But Nagle said he wouldn't let anyone else see—"

How about that? I was right about what had happened during the second part of the tape. But who was Nagle?

Hadley moved more and more into executive exasperation. "Look, whoever you are, you tell Nagle I can't pay more than twenty thousand. And I can't get the money together any faster, no matter how many of you he sends around. Tell him that and stay the hell away from me.'' He stepped around the car door and started to get behind the wheel.

I grabbed his arm just above the elbow and squeezed hard enough to wrinkle his fancy suit; muted gray in a conservative cut, very tasteful, eight hundred bucks if it was a dime.

''Hang on, Wally old pal,'' I said, ''we've had a change of plans here. You've hinted at so much interesting stuff, I've decided I *will* shoot you unless you settle down and tell all.''

Walter Hadley tried to pull his arm free. I squeezed harder. He tried one more time, then his face went tight and he stopped. He said, ''Oh, shit,'' in a small soft voice.

''Exactly,'' I said, and I let him get into his car.

Hadley slid across to the passenger side and I sat behind the wheel. I explained to him that I did not know what was going on but that I soon would. ''Just so there's no confusion, Wally,'' I said, ''the working definition of 'soon' is: before either of us gets out of this car.''

He nodded jerkily to show he believed me. Then we sat there while the Olds chewed up Hadley's expense account gas, the air conditioner blew soft cool air at us, and Wally-old-pal told me all the gory details.

CHAPTER THIRTEEN

Walter Hadley sat there, trapped in his own car, and looked out at the little park and its puny trees while he talked.

He was, as advertised, the head of Quality Control and Materiel Security at Dormac-Chaffee. Cricket Dawes had been his executive assistant. Apparently, up on the loftier rungs of the corporate ladder, secretaries were declassé. One didn't have a secretary; one had an executive assistant. Indeed one did.

I couldn't see the difference, but then I've never had a head for business.

To make a long story short—which Hadley did not do— one magic day it just happened. Their eyes misted over and their blood raced. Walter and Cricket had Fallen In Love. All caps, flashing neon, and don't spare the background music.

The way Walter Hadley described it, their red-hot romance was pretty blatant, but apparently Walter's wife hadn't noticed a thing. And she was still happily unaware.

After Hadley got into the story a little farther, the romantic aspect of the affair began to sound one-sided. Walter claimed Cricket doted on him; he admitted she taught him a whole batch of neat bedtime tricks. He didn't say why he needed the instruction. Maybe Walter-as-a-boy spent too much time in Business Administration 311 to get laid regularly.

No matter. The fact was, to Cricket the affair may have

been True Love, but on Walter's side, there was a big steamy slice of True Lust.

And that was the problem. After Walter knew all the tricks, it had become more and more inconvenient to steal the hours and evenings away from home so he could chase Cricket around her apartment with a feather duster and a can of Redi-Whip.

I'm only guessing about those details; he never specified feather dusters and Redi-Whip. Not exactly, anyway.

Regardless of the diversions, though, Walter had finally told Cricket he wanted to call off the affair. She did not think that was such a good idea.

"Actually," he said, "now I've had the opportunity to consider it, I see that while Cricket might have tried to break up with me eventually, she didn't want *me* to break up with *her*. Do you understand what I'm saying?"

"Yeah. I recall a similar problem with Sally Anne Kowalski just before the big homecoming game. She smeared ketchup on my letter jacket. Golly, what a mess." I smiled to show I'd finally gotten over it.

Hadley didn't like having his love life demeaned. He rubbed his sore arm and glared at a shiny new Pontiac cruising past us. There was a woman with a perfect hairdo behind the wheel and a sticker on the rear window that said: BORN TO SHOP.

"Don't get uppity with me, pal," I said. "If you hadn't kissed off your girlfriend, she probably wouldn't have tried to prove your company glows in the dark."

"What!" Hadley jumped. He was startled. But was it he-didn't-know-that startled or was it he-didn't-know-I-knew-that startled? Magnum or Spenser would have been able to tell right off, but I had no idea at all.

"Cricket had contacted an environmentalist group," I said. "She claimed you were losing radioactive stuff and leaking neutrons or whatever the hell you guys leak." Without mentioning The Green Army, I told him Cricket may have planned to steal incriminating files.

"Oh, no," Hadley groaned. Again, I couldn't tell whether he was upset because I knew or because he had not known.

He ducked the issue by returning to his affair with Cricket Dawes.

He said she had argued briefly about breaking up, then dropped the subject entirely. He said her office behavior had become stiff and formal. He knew she was angry, but he had no idea . . . etc. etc.

"Well, what about the things she claimed?" I said. "Is there anything wrong at the plant?"

Hadley shook his head, slowly and emphatically. It could have meant no or it could have meant no comment, but it definitely meant I was wasting my time on that angle.

"Okay," I said. "Then let's get back to the home porno movie"—he cringed like I'd hit him—"and you tell me when that was made."

"Four months ago," he said. "Perhaps five."

"Didn't like the idea much at first, did you?"

Hadley wouldn't look at me. "No."

"Why didn't you erase it?"

He shrugged. "I don't know. I intended to, but, well . . . We watched it sometimes. To get, uh, started. It was . . . exciting, in a way. And then after we weren't seeing each other, I forgot about it. Until Cricket died."

"Why didn't you just ask her for the video? You didn't have to kill her."

Hadley jumped like he'd been bitten by a snake. "No! Wait a minute, I didn't kill her! Oh, my God, you mustn't think—"

"Calm down," I said. "What did you do?"

He looked at me suspiciously for ten or fifteen seconds, then slumped back in his seat. "Oh, there's this private detective. Elmo Nagle. Well, he's not a real private detective. He doesn't have a license, but he used to be a police detective somewhere. He does things for people."

"I bet you ten bucks Nagle is short; about five six, five seven. Hundred-seventy pounds, more or less; anyway he's a chubby little bastard. Fiftyish. Eyebrows like caterpillars. And he smiles a lot. So how am I doing?"

"That's him. How did you know?"

"Never mind. Keep talking."

"What? Oh, well, I worried all weekend about that video.

I didn't know what the police might do or whether they'd
look in Cricket's apartment, but I knew someone would eventually pack up her things. Maybe the apartment manager,
maybe Cricket's family, I don't know who, but someone. I
felt I had to get that video before they found it.''

"And you hired Elmo Nagle, who 'does things for people.' ''

"That's right. Harv—uh, one of the men at the office had
some trouble with his daughter's boyfriend a few months ago.
He told me how to find Nagle."

"And?"

"And I contacted him and hired him to bring me the
video."

"Where does one find Elmo Nagle these days?"

"He doesn't have an office or a phone. I checked. The
only way to reach him is at a bar off Greenville Avenue. He
hangs around there with some pretty rough-looking friends.
I think some of them were carrying guns."

"Yeah," I said, "there's a lot of that going around. Just
for laughs, how much did you pay him?"

Hadley didn't consider it humorous. "One thousand dollars. In advance."

"And I gather that friend Nagle has decided blackmail is
even more lucrative than burglary."

Hadley signed. "Yes. He wants twenty thousand dollars,
or he says he'll mail a copy of the tape to Ann. My wife.
And another copy to the company."

"What are the payoff arrangements?"

"Why are you so sure I'm going to pay him?"

I looked at him awhile, and he finally said, "Nagle will
phone my office to tell me where to meet him. I don't know
exactly when, sometime in the next few days."

"There's no way to tell how many copies he might have
made," I said. "Paying Nagle off could become a monthly
occurrence. Had you thought of that?"

It's not often you see a man in an eight-hundred-dollar suit
look that miserable. "I've thought of it," Hadley said, "but
what can I do?"

"Well, Wally old pal, you're a pretty lucky guy. You're

also a jerk, frankly, but even jerks can have a good day now and then. You tell me everything you can about Nagle; his buddies, where he hangs out, all that stuff. Then I'll go whip the shit out of him and get the video for you.''

Hadley looked skeptical. ''Why do you want to get involved?''

''You don't need to know. You're making out all right.''

He wasn't reassured. ''It's money, isn't it? How much money will *you* want?''

''Not a dime, pal. This one's a freebie.''

''Why?''

''Rafferty's Rule Number Thirty-nine: Smiting the wicked sounds biblical, but mostly it's just good clean fun.''

CHAPTER FOURTEEN

I walked Hadley back through his story. That time, I asked for more details and took notes. Hadley did not enjoy the process. He was bored and irritable and long past being nervous when I finally let him leave. He drove away, late for work—hurry, hurry, things to do, harrumph. Arrogant bastard.

The morning had been very useful. The rest of my day was full of equally interesting bits.

"Nagle?" Ricco whined down the phone line. "Elmo Nagle? Jeez, I heard that name, but I can't . . . Lemme get back to you, Rafferty."

"I'm at my office," I said, "and I just want to tell you, Ricco, I've always appreciated the dedication shown by the thin blue line of the Dallas Police Department and its . . ." Why go on? Ricco had hung up by then.

I poured more coffee from the office percolator, reloaded the pipe, and sat with my feet on the desk, watching Honeybutt file things next door.

Honeybutt worked for an insurance agent whose office had been the newsroom back in the days when our building was a radio station. My office was the control room then. It was four feet higher and overlooked the newsroom through a double plate glass window almost six feet square.

I didn't have drapes on my side of that window, and Honeybutt almost never pulled the drapes on her side, especially when she filed things in the bottom drawers. Honeybutt was a world-class filer. Pretty good winker, too.

So far, we'd managed to avoid seeing each other in the hallway, which was good. Meeting her face-to-face or learning her real name would have ruined our relationship.

I tore myself away from one of Honeybutt's better moves— a half twist to the middle drawer, with a deft swirl of the hemline—and went back to work.

Despite the Sherlock Holmes trivia I'd spouted at Hilda, looking into Cricket's death was basic police work. Murder was always the simplest investigation, at least in the early stages. First, you check out the spouse and/or lover. Next, the family. Then, the victim's business connections.

Finally, and only as a last resort, look for a stranger who had killed during a robbery or at random. Every cop knew there were only two chances to find that stranger: slim and none.

But I had a much better chance because I didn't have to catch him. All I had to do was show that he existed, or even that he probably existed.

And all that would take was a few hours or days of basic police work.

It was a common sort of search I began; as ritualized as a church service or a restaurant meal. It started with the telephone. In my business most searches started with a telephone.

The voice was as canned as corn in January. "Dormac-Chaffee Energy Center, good morning."

"Personnel department, please."

"I'm sorry, sir, we do not maintain a separate personnel department. If you are seeking employment, you must—"

"This is Halperson from the Retail Credit Bureau," I said. "I want to verify employment on one of your people. Routine credit check."

"I see. In which department does the employee work?"

"I don't know. Her name is Dawes. Sandra Dawes."

"Oh. One moment, please."

She buzzed an extension. A man answered. His voice was impatient, irritated. "Yes, what is it?"

"Morning. Halperson, Retail Credit. I want to verify employment on Dawes, Sandra, for a loan application."

"Well, Mr. Halperson, it's a little late to be asking about Miss Dawes. She—"

Another voice, too far away from the phone for me to make out the words, interrupted him. The phone went hollow with the sound of a palm clamped over the mouthpiece. Then there were scrapes and bumps and whispers as the phone was passed hand to hand.

"Hello. May I help you?" The new voice was smooth and well controlled.

I went through the Halperson routine again and tried to inject a waspish, bureaucratic tone into the rendition.

"Miss Dawes no longer works here," said the man.

"Well, that *is* interesting, then. I'll have to bring this file up to date. Now, first of all, was she terminated or did she resign?"

My lightning serve didn't phase him. He returned it neatly. "Where did Miss Dawes apply for credit?"

"Oh, I wouldn't know that. I just get the yellow sheet from the internal 502 form and make the calls. Uh, who is this speaking?"

He waited exactly one beat, then said, "Jones."

"Right. Mr. Jones. I'll just make a note of that." We were so busy playing bullshit games with each other, neither of us was making any headway. "Now, Mr. Jones, what name did Dawes list as a medical emergency contact? You see, with a relative or friend's name, I can—"

"Mr. Halperson, I don't have that file in front of me at the moment. Suppose I check and call you back?"

"Well, I should turn in this report immediately."

"Yes, I understand," he said. "I won't be very long. Say, while you're there, what address do you have for Miss Dawes?"

Interesting. Whoever he was, he knew he didn't know all he wanted to know about Cricket Dawes.

"You don't have the address of your own employee?" I put a touch of clerkish sneer into it, just to show him what I thought of his record keeping.

"Mr. Halperson, if she falsely claimed to work here, who knows what address she might have given?"

He went too far that time. Foot fault, Dormac-Chaffee. Advantage, Rafferty.

"Wait a minute, Mr. Jones," I said. "Are you saying she *never* worked there?"

"No, I'm not saying that. She worked here. At one time."

Deuce. Damn.

"I see. Really, you should be careful about such allegations. Here at Retail Credit, we try to remain objective about these apparent anomalies which sometimes occur."

Weak volley.

"Certainly. However—"

"No, no. Mr. Jones, hear me out. You see, it is entirely possible this application predated her departure from your employ." I couldn't out-con him; maybe I could out-bore him. "Now, in such a case, we must assume—"

Badly hit lob. Uh-oh.

"I understand. Good-bye, Halperson," he said. "I'll call you back."

Smash. Advantage Dormac-Chaffee.

"Very well. The number is—"

"Never mind. I'll look it up." The line clicked dead.

Ace, Dormac-Chaffee. Game, Dormac-Chaffee. Rafferty fined for racket abuse.

It wouldn't take "Jones" more than ten minutes to prove what he already suspected; that "Halperson from Retail Credit" was a phony. I wondered if "Jones" was one of Dormac-Chaffee's security hotshots. But why were they playing it so close to the chest? Why waffle about something so easily checked as employment? And what was that business about her address? That sounded paranoid. Maybe they'd found out Cricket wasn't all she had seemed to be. How?

Hadley? When his affair with Cricket had started all this? No way!

So my first attempt to uncover Cricket's background left me with more questions and no answers.

You wouldn't believe how often that happens in this business.

Ricco called back at 12:27.

"Hey, I got some poop on this Nagle guy," he said. "Ed remembered. Nagle's an ex-cop. Not one of ours, thank Christ. He was suburban. Not Irving or Carrolton, either, but one of them places out west, we're not sure offhand. Anyway, Nagle and his partner busted a coke buy last year. Couple days later, the partner turned out to be more honest than he and Nagle thought. He 'fessed up that only half the coke had made it into the evidence locker."

"Now that's what I call trouble with a capital T."

"No shit," Ricco said. "But, see, that pissant suburban internal affairs department fucked up the investigation, and Nagle got away. They fired his ass; he didn't get away completely clean, but they didn't charge him, so that's as good as."

"Hey, thanks for this, Ricco. Do you know what Nagle is doing now?"

Ricco sniffed. "Word is, he's working your side of the street. Except he don't have a license, and half the time his 'clients' have more trouble, not less, after they hire him."

He paused. I could hear him sucking his teeth. "Look, Rafferty, I'm gonna take a chance here. I didn't know this until a couple of minutes ago, but there's an investigation running on Nagle. Blackmail. Some society dame in the Park Cities. It ain't my case, and frankly, it don't look too good. But do us a favor, will ya? Stay the hell out of the way."

"Ricco," I said, "would I impede a police investigation?"

"You heard me," he said, and hung up.

* * *

Hilda had a lunch meeting; Chamber of Commerce or Antique Dealers Cooperative or Good-looking Broads of Downtown Dallas; something like that.

I had two chili dogs and a couple of beers not far from the office, then strolled over to the police supply store to look at handcuffs. I halfway wanted an extra pair, but didn't see any I liked. Maybe Hilda would give me a set for Christmas.

Back to the office and back to work on the Life and Times of Cricket Dawes.

The current phone book had eight Dawes listings; from Chas R to Sharon. I phoned all of the Dawes numbers except Cricket's, looking for her relatives. Four of the seven answered. Wrong Dawes, they all said. I jotted down the three no-answers to try later.

Then I let my fingers do the walking down memory lane.

Hilda teased me sometimes because I had a great mound of old Dallas telephone directories in the corner of my office. She called them a dusty pile of wastepaper. I told her they were an edifice of priceless information. That's when she usually sniffed and flounced. I didn't care. Hilda did a helluva flounce.

Clients sometimes looked at all those phone books strangely, too. I told them my office was the Jackson Street collection point for the Boy Scout paper drive.

Dusty or not, ugly or not, those phone books were my version of a computer, thanks to Ma Bell and who knows how many pine forests.

Three minutes and four years back down the paper trail, I found where Cricket had lived before she moved into the Gaston Avenue apartment. A cross-check with the current Mapsco confirmed my guess that the address was a large apartment complex off Northwest Highway.

And the four-year-old phone book had even more interesting news. Six lines up from S. Dawes there was a listing for C. Dawes. They had the same address and phone number.

I had a few old Cole's reverse directories, too, and I tried the one closest to that year. Cole's had both phone numbers and agreed with Ma Bell about the address. Cole's wasn't so coy about the names. Sandra and Claire Dawes. Well, well, well.

Trekking ever backward, I found that Sandra and Claire had first shown up in the 1980 book. They weren't listed for 1979, but Dawes, Norman & Velma, were, with an address in a moderately up-market area between Abrams and Skillman, out near the LBJ Freeway.

I went back another fourteen years before I ran out of phone books. Norman and Velma Dawes were still there. They had moved once, upgrading houses by the look of it. There were other couples named Dawes that had once lived in Dallas, too. I made notes of their names and addresses, but I liked the look of Norman and Velma best of all. I bet myself the folks had retired to Florida or somewhere in 1979 and the daughters had stepped out on their own.

It's funny how once you're on a roll, everything seems to fall into place. I called the office of the apartment complex where Claire and Cricket had lived; the manager answered the phone. She remembered both Dawes girls. And she somehow had the idea I would interview her on television if she could impress me with her knowledge.

I cannot imagine why she thought that.

"Good girls, both of them," she trilled. "Not like some these days, with the drinking and the sex, and the Good Lord above only knows what drugs they take. Will I be on the evening news or that late one before Johnny comes on?"

Her name was Cartwright, and I pictured her as small and birdlike. A Helen Hayes stand-in, perhaps.

I said, "I'll have to talk to the producer about that, Mrs. Cartwright. When Claire and Sandra moved, where did Claire go?"

"Oh, didn't you know? Claire got married. To the nicest boy, too. Tall, blond young man. Will I have to wear a blue dress? I read somewhere that you have to wear blue on television."

"No, anything you want to wear is fine. What is Claire's married name?"

"Oh, my, you ask hard questions. Barker, Booker, something like that? Don't ask me that one on the TV; I don't want to seem foolish. My sister will be watching and she always says—''

"Please think, Mrs. Cartwright. Claire probably left you a forwarding address. For mail or a deposit refund. Can't you look it up?''

She giggled. It was schoolgirlish, except for a scary little bark at the end. "You haven't seen my bookkeeping, have you? Oh, my, I thought this was about poor Sandra. Why do you want to know all these things about Claire?''

I said, "Human interest. Suppose you were the person who located Sandra's relatives on live television? This could be very big, sympathywise. But if you'd rather not . . .''

"I really and truly need to find that address, do I?''

"Really and truly, Mrs. Cartwright. Sorry.''

"And no blue, you promise? I look terrible in blue.''

"No blue.''

"Well, wait a moment, then.''

It took her nine and a half minutes, and I heard her coming well before she fumbled for the receiver. "I got it!'' she said. "Jeff Borka.'' She spelled it for me. "That's the boy she married. He's Polish, I think, so don't you tell any of those jokes in front of him. Jeff's quite a nice boy, as I recall.''

Mrs. Cartwright had an address to go with the name. She offered to wait outside for the camera truck, but I told her not to do that because the boys were still trying to get it started.

"Oh, I won't,'' she said. "And, young man, you didn't really fool me with that TV story. But thank you so much for calling. It's been such fun!'' She hung up with a gentle click.

I'll be damned.

Ah, well, I'd looked foolish before and it hadn't hurt me. The good news was, I was finally getting somewhere.

I was stiff from sitting too long, and I stretched, long and lazily, enjoying the creak and pop of back and shoulders.

Just when I had my arms raised as high as I could get them, the office door opened. Two nattily dressed guys trying to look tough stepped into my office. Walter Hadley came in behind them.

"Hey, look here, Mr. Hadley," one of the sharpies said, looking at my raised arms. "He wants to give up already."

CHAPTER FIFTEEN

"As I recall," I said to Hadley, "this morning I offered to do you a big favor. Didn't you ever hear the one about gift horses and mouths?"

He smirked at me. "I was thinking more of shoes and other feet."

Hadley's two buddies watched this witty repartee without offering to join in. I wondered where Hadley found them and who they were. They looked too up-market smooth to be Nagle's leg breakers. And they were trying too hard to act like leg breakers to be Hadley's executive assistants. Which left . . .

"I give up, Wally old pal," I said. "Are these clowns company security or feebies?"

The youngest one was about twenty-three. He arranged his fuzzy cheeks into a scowl and said, "Who are you calling a retard, Rafferty?"

"No," I said wearily, "not feeb. *Feebie*. Fee-bie. F-B-I. Get it?"

They all looked blank.

"Never mind," I said, "you'd have to meet a few of them to understand." I clapped my hands and rubbed them briskly. "Okay! Now, to business. First, let's see some Dormac-Chaffee ID."

Would you believe it; the young one started to reach for his wallet!

The older one, thirty-fiveish with red hair, seemed about halfway competent. Red jabbed Junior with his elbow and frowned.

Hadley tried to live up to his take-charge image. He glared at me and grumped. Actually, it was a pretty fair grump. "Your juvenile humor fails to amuse, Rafferty," he said. "Why don't you just listen for a change?"

"Okay." I opened a desk drawer and reached inside it. Red and Junior were two full beats late. My hand was coming out of the drawer before their hands started under their suit coats.

I smiled at them and held up the paper clip from the drawer. They tried to turn their hand movements into scratches while I twiddled the paper clip around in the bowl of my pipe and removed a clot of horrible black gunk.

Now we all knew where we stood. I didn't (well, probably didn't) have a gun in the desk, and they did have guns under their coats. There were three of them, including Hadley, and they were standing. I was alone and seated.

But I was me and they were them, so I made the odds about even.

Hadley had been yammering something while his company goons and I were playing mind games. He blustered on. ". . . company matter. An internal company matter. There is no reason for interference by outsiders, especially private detectives and lunatic-fringe environmentalists. Do you understand me?"

"Hell, I didn't even hear half of that," I said, "but don't repeat it, please. I think you're saying I should lay off."

"Exactly. And I want to know which group hired you."

"No."

Red and Junior shuffled their feet. Hadley frowned. No one said anything for a while. Perhaps they found it difficult to deal with rejection.

Finally Hadley said, "Obviously you don't realize how much easier it will be for you if you agree to my suggestion."

"Maybe I can save us some time here," I said. "Let's

both assume you've already told me how much weight your company swings politically and how you can have my license lifted by noon tomorrow. And let's say you've also threatened me with bad credit ratings at every store in town, hourly visits from the building inspectors, and having the guy next door mow his lawn at five o'clock on Sunday mornings. None of that is good enough. What else you got?''

Hadley and Red looked thoughtful. Junior looked at each of them in turn, then decided to show those wimps who was the tough guy in the crowd. He said to me, ''How about a pair of broken legs, scuzz-bag?''

''My, my, what an original thought,'' I said. ''Don't waste your time, Junior. A lot better men than you have tried.''

Maybe being called ''Junior'' annoyed him. Maybe he wanted to show off for his bosses. Or maybe he just had suicidal tendencies. Anyway, his face went red and he pointed his right forefinger at me like a pistol barrel. ''It doesn't have to be you, tough guy. I bet you've got a wife or girlfriend, maybe kids—''

By that time I was around the desk and had Junior's finger bent back toward his wrist. I held it there while I said slowly, ''Think very carefully about what you just said to me.''

Then I broke his finger. It made a thin, sharp pop like a dry stick.

Junior gave a tight little shriek and dropped to his knees. He gingerly cradled his right hand against his chest and whined softly.

Red watched me warily. He had moved back, but only to give himself room. His right hand was inside his coat, low and held over toward his left hip. Unusual. You don't see all that many cross-draw hip holsters these days.

Hadley was plastered against the wall, white-faced and trembling. He kept saying, ''Wait a minute, wait a minute,'' over and over.

I sat on my desk and picked up the phone. ''We're even,'' I said to the three of them while I tapped out a number. ''For now.''

Mimi answered the phone and went to get Cowboy.

''Yo,'' he said.

"There's a company called Dormac-Chaffee out near Garland," I said. "Three employees are in my office right now, and they have grossly overstepped the bounds of good taste."

"Whoo-ee," Cowboy said. "You must really be pissed off. 'Overstepped the bounds of good taste.' You want me to whack 'em out for you?"

"Not yet. But if anything happens to a certain female friend of mine, anything at all, I'll be gunning for these three."

I spelled Hadley's name and gave Cowboy descriptions of the other two. Junior's finger still hurt too much for him to be tracking very well, but Hadley and Red seemed to see what was coming.

"Now, the problem is," I said to Cowboy, "this trio doesn't seem smart enough to fart and chew gum at the same time, but they might get lucky. If I'm not around, would you put their lights out for me?"

"Sure," Cowboy said, "be happy to. And can I have your chromed .38? 'Cause you wouldn't be needing it."

"You got it."

After I'd hung up, I said to Hadley, "Just in case there's any misunderstanding, let us define our relationship. You can come around here and try to mind-fuck me any time you want. Bring all the help you need, and we'll play your silly game by whatever rules seem appropriate at the time. We'll debate, arm-wrestle, trade six-inch jabs, or shoot, your choice. But if you—or any of your help—try to get to me through my loved one, we go straight to total war. I absolutely guarantee you would not live out the week. Got that?"

Hadley nodded. Actually, his head moved like it was attached to a telegraph key, but it was closer to nodding than to anything else.

"These two," I said, pointing at Junior and Red, "do they know about the other thing?"

Hadley's eyes became even more round. "No, uh, I . . . ."

"Okay. I still intend to do what I said this morning."

"But—"

"Go away," I told them. "Get the hell out of here."

They looked back several times as they left. And Junior

bumped his hand on the door frame, the clumsy fool. Boy, could he scream!

I slammed the door behind them and looked around the office. I was still hyped-up and buzzing. I didn't know whether I wanted coffee, booze, sleep, or a rubber room.

Then I saw Honeybutt's face through the plate glass window. She was sitting at her desk, staring up into my office. Her mouth and eyes made three perfect circles.

I winked at her. She didn't wink back.

I started to make coffee, then decided I didn't want coffee. I dialed Claire Borka, née Dawes, and got a busy signal. I looked at Honeybutt and she looked away.

Aw, the hell with it.

I went home, and found a surprise package on the front steps.

CHAPTER SIXTEEN

Linda Taree, the Green Army receptionist, sat on my steps with her sneaker-clad feet on the concrete walk. By Green Army standards, she was formally dressed; she wore jeans and a black long-sleeved blouse with a high neckline. A row of white buttons marched down the front of the blouse.

A fringed leather bag or purse with beaded Indian designs on it lay beside her feet. In front of my house a weary Volkswagen Beetle leaned against the curb and invited passersby to read its stickers and update their social consciences.

Linda didn't look up until I stopped in front of her. She had done something extra to her hair. The red curly entanglement was more bulbous than before, which made her face seem even narrower. For the first time, I realized she had green eyes.

"To repeat myself," I said, "I'm sorry about yesterday. If I'd known that particular nerve was so sensitive, I wouldn't have scraped it."

"It's okay. When I calmed down, I realized you didn't mean it that way." She shrugged. "Age difference, I guess."

"Meaning the old fart didn't know what he was doing?"

She grinned. "Now I'm doing it, huh?"

"I'm not sure. Are you?"

"Maybe. I'm not sure, either." She picked up her bag and stood. "May I come in?"

"That depends. Are you going to play grab-ass again? Because I'm more than just a superbly fit and tantalizing body, you know."

She rolled her eyes nd showed me that rueful grin again. "No. I'll be good."

Inside, I offered her a drink. She asked for white wine, which I didn't have, then she tried for a Coke and caught me with my inventory down again. I suggested coffee. She countered with hot tea. I didn't have that, either.

We finally settled on ice water for her and Scotch for me, after five minutes of being so goddamned nice to each other it was sickening.

I waved her to the sofa in my living room, took the chair opposite and decided to get my licks in before we had another fight. "Tell me about Cricket Dawes," I said.

She looked surprised at first, then smiled. "I thought you told Jim all about Cricket Dawes yesterday."

"Not really. I told Winchester what he didn't know about her. I'd like to hear what you do know."

That brought narrow wrinkles of suspicion to her eyes. "Exactly what are you talking about?"

"Your impressions of her. As a person. Don't be so damned defensive."

"Oh. Umm, she was shallow, I think. Too busy looking for Mister Right, the simple bitch."

I said, "Now, now. Mustn't be bitter."

She sipped her water and grimaced. "How will women ever . . . Oh, I just get so damned sick of that type, you know, with their pretty little office dresses and beauty parlor appointments and eye shadow and lipstick and mascara and all that crap."

"Cricket was a touch overdone, was she?"

Linda shrugged. "Well, not theatrical, if that's what you mean. But, hey, look, I'm not a good judge. To me, *any* makeup is too much."

"How many times did you meet Cricket face-to-face?"

"Only once, which is not enough, considering how I just dumped on her, right? I'll give you that one. I met her once and talked to her on the phone two or three times. Three, I think.''

"When and where did you meet her?"

"About a week after she first contacted us. In the shoe department of the Neiman-Marcus store at Prestonwood. I picked up her first information drop.''

"Somehow I don't see you fitting in at Neiman's.''

She giggled. "No way! But that was the idea, see? It was part of Jim's security plan. He thought nobody would expect us to use a bourgeois place like that as a rendezvous. Good, eh?''

"Great," I said. Well, we were getting along fairly well. Why rock the boat? "What information did Cricket give you?''

"Crap, mostly. An organization chart, as I remember, and a lot of office gossip and rumors.'' Linda put her glass down on the side table and leaned forward with her elbows on her knees. "You might be able to understand the problem. Most people can't, for some reason. You see, these days the companies fight back. We must have hard information to stop them. We can't go public with theories anymore; the mass media won't use a story unless we can prove what the polluters and poisoners are up to.'' She smiled. "Sorry. I get worked up. But you see the point. And Cricket didn't have any hard information that time.''

"What did she say when you told her that?''

"Actually, I didn't tell her. Tom and I went through her material, then Tom phoned her that night. He told me about it later. He said Cricket sounded disappointed and promised to do better. She intended to get the files concerning radiation leaks.''

"That's what Winchester told me. But are you sure there really were—or are—leaks?''

"Of course there are!'' She stopped then, and started again more slowly. "I'll be absolutely objective here. There have been rumors for months about leaks at Dormac-Chaffee, but so far there is no proof. As far as I know.''

"And you can hear a rumor about anything,'' I said.

"True.'' It was a long, reluctant admission despite the

promise to be objective. Then the excitement of the chase got to her and she rushed on. "But you see how great it would be if we could prove it! Really nail those bastards for dumping their nuclear garbage on the world. That's what Cricket might have done for us."

"But she didn't, did she?"

"No," she said, "she didn't." She almost said something else, but stopped herself. She leaned back on the sofa and finger-combed her springy hair. "Anyway, that's not your problem, is it? The way I hear it, you're supposed to prove Dormac-Chaffee killed her."

"That's what Winchester wanted, but things are a tad more logical now. I'm trying to find out *who* killed her. There's a big difference."

"Oh, you've finished already?" she said archly.

"Point taken," I said. "There *may* be a difference. In any case, let's work on it before Winchester's money runs out. When you met Cricket at Neiman's, was she alone?"

"Yes."

"You're certain? Did you see her come into the store? Or did you look up and find her standing next to you?"

"I saw her several minutes before we spoke. At least five minutes before. Neither of us was quite sure who we were meeting, I guess. Anyway, she came alone. And she left alone, too."

"What did you two talk about?"

"Nothing, really. She said, 'I'm Cricket.' Kind of hesitantly, you know? I said, 'Hi. I'm Linda,' and she handed me an envelope full of papers. A letter-sized envelope, not one of those big ones. Then she said good-bye and left. I pretended to shop for ten minutes or so, then I left, too."

"What time of day was that?"

"Twelve-fifteen, twelve-thirty, something like that. It would have been her lunch hour. She acted like it was, anyway. She seemed to be in a hurry to leave once she'd given me the envelope."

"Or she could have just been nervous. That spy stuff might upset an amateur."

Linda eyed me cautiously, then shrugged her thin shoulders. "Maybe. One or the other."

"Okay, you didn't talk about anything during that meeting. What about on the telephone? Any girlish confidences exchanged?"

Linda Taree started to bristle. I held up both hands. "All right, I'm sorry. I retract 'girlish.' I'm interested in anything she might have said about her friends, that's all. Especially male friends."

She seemed to give me the benefit of the doubt, perhaps because of my advanced age and mental rigidity. "No, I don't remember anything like that. Mostly, she asked about the specific material we needed. Each time, she asked me to repeat things, like she was taking notes. Then she'd say, 'Thank you,' and we'd hang up." A pause for thought, then: "You know, she seemed to treat the whole thing as a chore. Just another job to do."

"So she wasn't enthusiastic about it?"

"Oh, she was enthusiastic, I guess, but she wasn't . . . I guess she wasn't committed like the rest of us."

"Did she ever seem frightened or worried about what she was doing?"

"No. Very cool woman. Wait, that's not quite right. It makes her sound uninterested. I think businesslike is the best word. Yes, businesslike."

Speaking of business . . .

"Did Cricket ever mention the name Walter Hadley?" I asked.

"Not that last name, but, hey, she worked for a guy named Walter. I don't think she liked him. She said something once, what was it, something like, 'It'll be fun to take the files out from under old Walter's nose.' That's not quite it, but you get the idea."

"Okay," I said, "thanks. Now, since Tom talked to her, too, he might be able to tell me more. Do you know where I can phone him tonight?"

"Forget it. Tom's gone."

"Gone? Where?"

She laughed bitterly. "It got real exciting after you left

yesterday. Jim went out of his skull. He got after Tom and me; kicked our butts for letting him down."

"That was my fault," I said. "I rubbed his nose in it, and he needed an outlet. Sorry."

"Don't sweat it. Jim can be a real ass at times. The point is, he pulled us off the Dormac-Chaffee project and took over himself. He's got all our notes and files and everything. And he sent Tom to Matagorda Island to do a sandhill-crane survey or some such bullshit. Busywork, that's all."

"And Tom went, just like that?"

"Hey, if you were nineteen years old and thought Jim Winchester was God, you'd go, too." She shook her head. "Jim told me to go with Tom." She grinned wickedly with the memory of it.

"And what did you say to that?"

Linda sat upright, turned sideways on the sofa, and beamed a grotesque smile over her shoulder. In an exaggerated southern accent, she said, "Wal, sir, ah smiled real purty-lak and ah sayed, 'Fuck you very much, Doctuh Winchestah!' "

She melted out of her pose and flopped bonelessly against the sofa back. "Then I walked out."

"I see. Are you just AWOL for the day, or have you deserted for good?"

"I don't know yet," she said. "It depends."

She developed an intense interest in her left knee, tracing small circles on her faded jeans with one finger. I dropped my head onto my chair back and watched a spider on the ceiling build a web monument to my casual housekeeping. I yawned and wondered how I could be so tired for the little physical exercise I'd had that day.

Then the *scritch-scritch* of Linda's fingernail ended, and I raised my head to look at her. She had a bright, glitzy smile plastered on her thin face.

"Hey," she said, "I've got this problem. Maybe you can help me."

"Uh-huh," I said.

"I feel bad about groping you the other day, but I can't think of how to apologize properly without sounding like some teenage virgin."

"You already have. Don't worry about it."

"No," she said, "that's not fair. You didn't let me work it out."

"Oh."

"You don't understand, do you?"

"No," I said, "apparently not."

"This is really dumb. See, I want to go to bed with you, but I don't know exactly how to ask you. Or maybe I don't want to have to ask. I'm not sure which."

I drained the last of my now-watery Scotch and crunched an ice cube. Finally, I said, "Well, you see, that's not as easy as—"

"You're telling me!" she said. "Wow, this is weird. Most guys your age—sorry about that—anyway, they get all smarmy and oily and they come on to *me*. But you're kind of— Oh, hey, are you gay? Because I'm sorry if—"

"No. But I am committed. Sorry."

Her grin got broader and more false. "Committed? Bed, too? Is that what she says?"

"That's what I say."

"Hey, you don't know what you're missing. Everybody says I give great head."

"I'm sure that's true, but . . ."

"Yeah," she said, leaping up and striding for the door. "Well, hell, I don't need a goddamn building to fall on me. I just thought—"

She whirled to face me as I stood up, too. "Look, Rafferty," she said sternly, "I don't know whether I'm going back to work for Jim or not, but I'm still interested in this Dormac-Chaffee thing. I'd like to see how it turns out. That's why I figured if we . . . anyway, can we sort of keep in touch? Ah, bad choice of words there. What I mean is—"

"Sure. Give me a call. I'll tell you what I can."

She nodded shortly and stalked out the front door. Her VW whined and whirred and finally burst into a series of pops and blats that slowly faded as she drove away.

The ship's clock Hilda gave me last Christmas bonged four times. Four bells; six o'clock. I went to the phone and tapped buttons.

Hilda answered, sexily short of breath. She had just arrived home and run in from the garage.

"Babe," I said, "you are not going to believe all the weird stuff that happened to me today."

CHAPTER SEVENTEEN

"But why would this Hadley character want to harass you?" Hilda said. She broke a breadstick and nibbled at it.

"I can only guess, but there could be several reasons. Maybe he's changed his mind and thinks it's safer to pay off Nagle than to have me get the video; maybe Cricket really did get away with company files and he's afraid I'll find them; maybe he's just pissed off because I scared him this morning." I couldn't think of any other reasons offhand, so I forked my spaghetti carbonara and carefully twirled the next bite into a perfect sphere.

"Don't worry about Hadley throwing his weight around," I said. "He's having second thoughts now."

The ball of spaghetti held its shape and let me eat it without dangling down over my chin. I chewed happily, swallowed, then told Hilda about Junior's big mouth and what it had earned him.

"You broke his finger?" She looked slightly ill.

"Yeah. Well, it wasn't what you'd call an authorized threat, but sometimes jerks like that will try to run with a bad idea and . . . Anyway, I got their attention and I set the ante too high. And besides, Junior was only fishing. They don't even know you exist."

"They found you pretty fast."

"Hadley would have seen my license plate when I braced

him this morning. It wouldn't take too long to run me down from there. Finding you is different, even if they wanted to, and they don't. Especially now. Anyway, I'll be with you tonight and after work tomorrow; we'll be gone over the weekend; you're out of town next week running down antiques in St. Louis. No problems.''

"Uh-huh," Hilda said. She gave that look. "You've gotten yourself quite involved this time, haven't you?"

"Me?" I said. "It's just another case, babe."

"You say that, but I think that poor woman, um, Cricket, bothers you," Hilda said. She smiled to show me she was only interested, not complaining.

I chewed an overly large mouthful of spaghetti and thought about that. "Guilty," I said finally. "It's odd, Hil. Cricket Dawes was so many of the things I dislike in people. She was silly enough to mess around with a married man. Granted, it might have been a serious relationship to her, but it wasn't to him, and she should have known that. Plus, when he dumped her, she tried to hurt him through his job. She was sneaky instead of having it out with him face-to-face. To look at her apartment, she didn't seem to enjoy much. She didn't read, she didn't have any apparent hobbies, except Wally, and she had a . . . oh, a sort of glitzy air about her.

"But," I said, "nobody deserves to die the stupid, almost accidental, way she did. I feel sorry for her. Really sorry." I shrugged, a little embarrassed now. "I even feel a little bit close to her, which I cannot understand at all."

Hilda laced her fingers together and rested her chin on them. She smiled at me gently. "You don't have to apologize for feeling compassion. And as for feeling close to her, you went through her apartment. That's like looking inside her head. At least, I think it is. When that burglar got my TV set last year, I felt violated just knowing a stranger had wandered through my house."

Hilda reached over and patted my hand. "Relax, Rafferty, sometimes you worry too much about being tough. It's all right to admit you're an old softie inside."

"What if my neighborhood chapter of the Young Republicans finds out?" I said. "They're pretty hard-nosed about softies. They have this ceremony where they tear off your NRA badges and—''

Hilda laughed. ''Tell you what, bucko, the Young Republicans could get you on at least two counts. Isn't their retirement age thirty or something?''

''You may think me ancient, woman, but many females find me irresistible, despite my advanced age.'' I told her about my afternoon session with Linda Taree.

When I'd finished, Hilda said, ''Thank you, Rafferty.'' She shook her head thoughtfully. ''I do not understand people like that. Her idea of fun sex sounds like two dogs in an alley.''

''Aw, be nice, babe. You should feel sorry for her. She's probably never had what we have. So she chases it too hard.''

''As long as she chases someone else, pal. As long as she chases someone else.''

After the meal, we both ordered brandy and coffee. I loaded and lit my pipe, then looked out through a cloud of smoke to find Hilda staring at me.

''Tell me something,'' she said. ''Suppose those men—all of them, not just the young one whose finger you broke— suppose they had been serious about hurting me. What would you have done then?''

''I'd have killed them. What else?''

''But you can't just go around . . . Rafferty, that's sweet, but don't you see that . . . I mean—''

''Reverse the roles, babe. Suppose they planned a nasty experience for me. What would you do?''

Hilda looked puzzled, then thoughtful, then irritated. ''Oh, shut up and drink your coffee.''

I shut up and drank my coffee.

CHAPTER EIGHTEEN

Thursday morning. Nine-thirty. Chaos.

Claire Borka, née Dawes, Cricket's sister, was thirtyish and pale. Not pale as in Hilda's old line about "pale and interesting," but pale as in sickly or exhausted. Under the circumstances, though, pale was understandable. Claire Borka was mothering three small children, supervising a Bekins crew moving furniture out of her house, and sliding rapidly toward a nervous breakdown.

"Ronny!" she shrieked, and darted toward an open-topped wooden cage in the corner of the empty living room. In the cage a small boy in lumpy red overalls drooled cheerfully while he chewed on a cat's tail. The cat didn't seem to mind much, but Claire Borka was pretty upset about it.

"Oh, Ronny." She shooed the cat away and scrubbed the kid's lips with a tissue from her skirt pocket. "Look, Mr. Rafferty," she said over her shoulder, "I don't have time to talk, honestly."

"I can see that," I said, "and I'll be as quick as possible, but it is very important."

She turned around and half sat on the corner of the cage thing. I knew there was a name for those gadgets, but I couldn't think of what it was.

"I've already told the police everything," she said wearily. "Isn't that enough?"

"Please, Mrs. Borka," I said. "Just tell me if Cricket had any romances or affairs with men you think might have been likely to harm her."

Claire dragged the back of her hand across her forehead. "But I already . . . Oh, all right. Mr. Rafferty, I haven't—hadn't—seen my sister for three months. We talked on the phone once or twice a week, though, and we were . . . oh, I suppose we were as close as most sisters our age. I mean, it wasn't like high school, but—wait a minute!"

One of the movers had walked through the living room carrying a large modern painting. Claire said to him, "That one has to be crated. I forgot to tell you before. Sorry.'

The man shrugged and took the painting back toward wherever he'd found it. Claire Borka turned her blank face back toward me. She looked terrible. "You want to know the worst part?" she said. "I haven't had time to cry yet. What with this stupid move and the company wanting Jeff early and the kids and all, I still don't know Cricket's gone. I mean, I know it, but . . ." She dropped her chin and watched her fingers pick at the soggy tissue. Her nails were ragged.

After a few minutes, I said gently, "Boyfriends?"

"Oh, right. No, I don't think she went out with anybody like that." Behind her, the kid clumsily stomped around the perimeter of his corral gizmo. What the hell was the name for those things?

"Mrs. Borka, can you tell me where to reach your parents?"

She shook her head rapidly, doggedly. "You can't," she said. "There was an accident. A car accident, a long time ago."

Two small children, three or four years years old, ran clumsily through the room. The boy chased the girl. He pointed a black plastic ray gun and made loud spluttering noises with his lips. The girl screamed in delight. Claire Borka and I watched them go past.

"What kind of a girl was Cricket, Mrs. Borka? Was she interested in politics or the conservation movement, anything like that?"

"Cricket?" Claire sniffed and mechanically wiped her nose with the same tissue she had used to scrape cat off her son's mouth. "No," she said, "Cricket wasn't interested in that sort of thing."

"Did she ever talk about her work or what they did at that plant? Was she worried about the work or her safety?"

"She didn't split atoms, for crying out loud. She worked in an office. What's to worry about in an office?"

A mover came hesitantly into the room. "Excuse me," he said. "Uh, about that hall closet . . ."

Claire sighed and slowly lifted her backside off the corner of the cage. "Look, I've got things to do."

"Last question," I said. "Did Cricket give you anything to hold for her? A package? Or an envelope? It would have happened sometime in the last month."

Claire Borka shook her head. "No. Nothing. In fact, I haven't even gotten her things out of her apartment. With Jeff already in Portland and . . . I wanted to, but I couldn't."

The mover cleared his throat. Claire said, "Yes. I'm coming." They walked out of the room.

The little boy in the cage and I looked at each other. "How about it, kid," I said, "what do you call that thing you're in?"

A voice behind me said, "It's a playpen. You never heard of a playpen before?" One of the movers lugged a cardboard box out the far door, still muttering to himself.

The kid grinned from ear to ear. Then he noisily threw up all over himself. Then he grinned again.

Claire Borka, in the back of the house, said, "Oh, no, Ronny! Please, not again!" Rapid female footsteps headed toward the living room.

The toddlers made another screaming pass through the room and out a different door this time.

Crockery crashed in the kitchen. There was a soft curse, then a man's voice called out, "Mrs. Borka? Gotta little problem here."

Me, I got the hell out of there.

* * *

"What can I tell you?" he said. "It was like losing a daughter." Stanley Mellish was the manager of the Casa Cahuenga. He was bald and late forties. He was also triangular, with narrow sloping shoulders, a big butt, and barrels for legs.

"Hey," he said, "you know how these places are. It's only luck if you get good tenants. And I'll tell you the truth, I got a few in here I wouldn't mind seeing leave. But not poor Cricket."

Mellish had large doughy hands with fat white fingers. As he talked, his hands rubbed and prodded, thumped and chased each other around the counter in his little office near the Casa Cahuenga front entrance.

"Tell me about her," I said.

"Nice girl," Mellish said. "A real nice girl. Kept a beautiful apartment. No problem. Cheerful, too. Always said hello or waved. Pleasant. That's the word, Mr. Rafferty. Cricket was a pleasant girl."

I had given Mellish my real name, mostly because I couldn't remember the phoney name I'd used the night I burgled Cricket's apartment. It didn't seem to matter. Now, late in the morning, the Casa Cahuenga was all but deserted.

I smiled chummily at Mellish. "Did Cricket have any special friends who visited her often?"

Mellish shook his head slowly. "I don't keep track of my tenants' friends," he said. "What do you think I am?"

"I think you're a friend of Cricket's," I said. "And a real friend, a dedicated friend, would help me find whoever did that terrible thing to her."

Sometimes in my work I have to invent the craziest bullshit you ever heard.

Mellish looked very serious. His hands scampered around the counter like fat crabs on speed. He finally bought it. "Well, there was only one man, but I saw him several times."

He described Walter Hadley and his visits to Cricket's apartment. Stanley Mellish was pretty sharp; his recollection of when and how often Hadley visited Cricket agreed with Hadley's version. I wrote all that down like it was hot news.

"Good," I told Mellish. "I'll check it out. Now, what about friends here in the building? Let's just say that Cricket had something valuable she wanted to leave with a friend. Whom would she pick?''

Mellish's crab-hands shifted into top gear. ''What an odd way to ask,'' he said. ''Why, I don't know exactly.'' The crabs did a shoulder-high back flip and landed on the counter again. ''We weren't close or anything, but since you mentioned leaving a package, why, I suppose the answer is me,'' Mellish said. ''A year ago, Cricket went to Mexico for two weeks. She left her good jewelry and silver with me. Is that the sort of thing you mean?''

''Yeah. Has she ever asked you to hold anything else? Papers, envelopes, a box?''

''No. Nothing.'' The crabs performed unnatural acts upon each other.

''Have you been through her apartment yet?''

''Oh, no! The police were very explicit about that. No one is allowed in until they say so. In fact, Cricket's sister wanted to get her clothes and things. I had to say no, which was a shame, I thought.''

I thought so, too. Nothing seemed to be going right for Claire Borka this week.

Mellish and the crabs beckoned me closer for a conspiratorial conference. ''*Someone* may have gotten in, though,'' Mellish said. ''Monday night we had a prowler, but Frank Mulock—he's in thirty-two—swears it was really a burglary. He says he saw the burglar come out of Cricket's apartment and . . .''

Then I had to listen to Mellish tell me a wildly distorted version of my botched burglary. I had to write it down, too.

Of course, it wasn't all bad. The way Mellish told it, I was larger than life in every way. I was stronger than Arnold Schwarzenegger and faster then Carl Lewis. I could fight like a tiger and disappear like a chameleon.

I was very impressed by me.

I finally left the Casa Cahuenga about noon, strutting just a little, and found a phone to check with my answering service.

Walter Hadley had phoned every thirty minutes all morning,

the girl said. He left the same message each time. ''Nagle meeting tonight. Call me. Urgent.''

How about that? Now I had a chance to live up to Mellish's star billing.

CHAPTER NINETEEN

Eleven o'clock on a Thursday night was not the best time to boogie with the Beautiful People. Not that the timing mattered; Beautiful People didn't boogie at bars like the one where Nagle hung out.

It was a dump named Fulvio's. The building had been around a long time; it had been renovated and added on to three times too many. The place was strangely shaped, and there were several floor levels inside, each level only one or two steps higher or lower than the others. It was an ideal bar for people who liked to get drunk and fall down a lot.

Cowboy and I sat at the bar and watched Nagle in the mirror over the bottles. He was thirty feet behind us, sitting at a table with three other men.

"He don't look so goddamn bad," Cowboy said. "And he took that cassette thing away from you without a fight?"

"You had to be there," I said.

I lifted my chin toward Nagle and his friends in the mirror. "I make the guy in the red shirt as an outsider. One of Nagle's customers, maybe. The other two must be muscle. They're working too hard at looking bored to be anything else."

"Reckon you're right," Cowboy said. "So what—"

"Par'n me, honey," a strident voice said to Cowboy,

"but ain't you that movie guy, James Coburn, Colburn, or somepin?" She was a bleary-eyed blonde with more make-up than all the Gabors put together. Her age wasn't far off all the Gabors put together, either. "C'mon, thass you, right?"

Cowboy started to argue with her, then saw me rolling my eyes at the bar mirror. He scrawled James Coburn's autograph on a cocktail napkin and gave it to the sozzled blonde.

"Thas awful sweet, Jimmy," she said. "Hey, I loved that thing you did with the knife throwing. *Zuupppp!* You remember that, in the old cowboy pitcher with the bald guy? That movie where you didn't hardly say anything?" She beamed a toothy smile at him. Her eyes slowly crossed, then un-crossed with a snap.

"Bye-bye, Jimmy," she said, and backed away, wag-gling her fingers at Cowboy. She stumbled on the steps down to the next level and almost fell. A beefy guy in a plaid shirt caught her arm and eased her into a chair at his table. When Cowboy and I turned back to our beers, the beefy guy was leaning over the old blonde, honking her left breast like the mute Marx brother used to honk that silly horn.

Fulvio's was that kind of a bar.

"Damn," Cowboy said, "I hate it when people ask me that. I don't really look like that Coburn guy, do I?"

"Of course you do," I said. "When he was younger, though."

Cowboy sighed and sipped his beer. "Okay, boss man, what now?"

"We've found Nagle and his helpers, so let's get out before he recognizes me. Unless you'd rather circulate amongst your fans; maybe sign a few more autographs?"

Cowboy stood up and adjusted his Stetson. "Man thinks he's funny," he said to the ceiling. "Ha-ha. Wait'll he sees my bill for this pissant little hog-tying contest."

Behind Cowboy, his blond fan howled with loud, brittle laughter. The beefy guy was honking both her breasts then. He laughed, too.

* * *

East Lawther Drive was a complicated road in White Rock Lake Park. It jumped and skittered through the park in a series of disjointed segments. It was a great street for certain things, especially at night.

Most of those things could get you into trouble of one sort or another, but that didn't slow anyone down. In fact, the only problem was in finding an empty spot for whatever excitement you had in mind.

"Will you look at that?" Cowboy said, as we rumbled past a parked van with a desert sunset painted on its side. "Perfectly good truck all gee-gawed up just so some kids got a comfy place to neck."

"You're just jealous because you had to go parking on horseback when you were that age," I said.

"Hah! You city kids never did find out about using a pickup bed and a coupla armloads of hay."

"True. Hey, I remember one girl—Elise, her name was—and one night when we were out in her mother's VW—"

Cowboy tugged his hat even lower on his forehead. "Oh, my, this sure is fun," he said, "riding around in the middle of the night with an armed, horny, nostalgia freak."

"In a stolen truck," I said. "Don't forget that part in your memoirs."

Cowboy had swiped a dusty one-ton Jimmy with four-wheel drive for the evening's sport. The big Jimmy was a kidney banger; it bumped and jolted and grumbled along with all the finesse of a rock slide. And it felt as unstoppable as a rock slide, too, which was the whole idea.

Nagle had told Hadley to drive up and down the segment of East Lawther that ran south from Northwest Highway. That section had more than its fair share of loops, half-circular diversions, and side roads. It even had an escape hatch, where access roads led to and from Mockingbird Lane.

Nagle was a pretty good tactician. He and his goons would

sit somewhere along that stretch of East Lawther, probably out of sight, and watch Hadley look for them. When they were sure he wasn't dragging a convoy of cops, they would flash their headlights three times—oh, boy, oh boy, a secret code!—and Hadley was supposed to stop and swap the twenty grand for the video.

That's the way Nagle had it figured; clean, quick, and almost foolproof.

But then again, Nagle hadn't figured on Cowboy and me.

"How we doing for time?" Cowboy asked. He drove with his head tilted back a fraction so he could see out from under the lowered brim of his big hat.

"According to Nagle's Plan A, Hadley should be starting his first pass in ten minutes," I said. "I figure Nagle and his boys are already here."

"Yup."

Cowboy and I were on our third pass then. We were getting a feel for the park and its occupants.

"It's either the silver Pontiac down by the water or that Buick in the bushes up toward Northwest and Buckner," I said.

"Prob'ly. You ready to move now? Too boring just riding around. Let's kick us some ass."

"Onward," I said, making a wagons-ho motion. "Excelsior!"

"Whyn't you talk English?"

"Better yet, I'll translate. 'Excelsior' is Latin for 'kick ass.' "

"Figgered it was somethin' like that."

We looked for the Pontiac first. It was gone. Ten yards from where it had been parked, there was a man pawing around in the opened trunk of an old Chevrolet. The car was one of those Impalas from the 1960s; slab sided and at least thirty feet long. The guy was bent over with his hands out of sight. He was putting something together or taking it apart.

"Well now, looky here," Cowboy said. He stopped the truck and flipped on two spotlights the Jimmy's owner had thoughtfully bolted to the top of the cab.

The Impala and the man behind it were nailed by the light beams. He turned and brought out a hand to shield his eyes. He held something in the other hand, but it was still masked by his body and the car trunk.

Cowboy's door clicked softly as he popped the latch but held the door closed to keep the interior light off. I did the same thing.

"Do I detect a certain suspicion of your fellow man?" I said.

"You sure do talk purty at times, Rafferty. I hadn't thought about them putting a hitter by the side of the road to whack out your friend and take the payoff money. Did you?"

"No. Can you see what he's got in the trunk there?"

"No. Ain't that some coincidence?"

Ahead of us, the man squirmed and peered into the spotlights and high beams. He was twentyish, which was young but not unheard of for a hitter. He wore faded jeans and a light-colored long-sleeved shirt. Lousy clothing for an after-dark hit. And the thing in his right hand was shiny, which didn't sound like a night weapon. Still . . .

"Don't mind us," Cowboy yelled to the man. "Just thought you might need some light."

After a few seconds, the man waved and turned his back to us. He lifted his whatsit out of the trunk.

It was a saxophone.

The Jimmy's doors chunked shut at the same instant. "Well, hell," Cowboy grumbled, "you got to play all the angles." I tried to lean my shotgun casually against the seat so Cowboy wouldn't notice I had picked it up.

Then I saw him trying to pull the same scam on me.

Up near the Impala, the young musician hooked his sax onto his neck strap and began tootling scales.

Cowboy killed the spotlights and we started moving again. As we passed the sax player, he was strolling off the road, down toward the water's edge, ragging and vamping around "Basin Street Blues."

I thought he sounded pretty good. I'd have to bring Hilda out sometime to listen to him practice.

"Good thing we didn't whack him," I said. "Not enough people play trad jazz these days. We can't afford to lose any."

"The Buick must be the one, then," Cowboy said, shifting up a gear. "How you want to do it?"

"The direct approach, I think. That suit you?"

Cowboy grinned sardonically. "Suits me right down to the ground, boss man."

CHAPTER TWENTY

Cowboy kept the Jimmy tooling along about thirty as we approached the place where we'd last seen the Buick. It had been tucked away about twenty feet off the pavement then, at a right angle to the road, beside a large thicket. We were moving in on the Buick's exposed flank.

As soon as we caught the first faint glimpse of body metal in the headlights, Cowboy manhandled the truck off the pavement, angling cross-country toward the parked Buick. The Jimmy leaped and crashed through the shrubbery. It was a rough, noisy trip.

"Lights!" Cowboy bellowed.

After two tries in the bucking, swaying cab, I found the switch and turned on the overhead spotlights. The Buick-shape ahead exploded into clarity. It was long, shiny, and maroon, I saw. Pretty color.

Two startled faces, one of them Nagle's, and a third vague man-shape were visible. A hand with a pistol in it waved briefly.

"Go!" I hollered over the engine racket and the rattle of things bouncing around under the seat.

Cowboy floored it. The engine noise got louder.

About ten yards from the Buick, we hit a small ditch. The front end bounced in and out violently. The rear end hung up briefly, then the big Jimmy waddled clear, still aimed at all that tender Buick sheet metal.

The rear door of the Buick opened about two feet, but whoever opened it changed their mind and didn't jump out.

That indecision cost them their only chance to get away.

We hit the Buick at a fair clip and shunted it sideways five or six feet. Cowboy yelled something—"Yahoo" or something rodeoish like that—and he stirred the gear and drive levers until he found the lowest gear in the box. The Jimmy grunted.

It really did. That big truck grunted and pawed the ground with all four wheels, and it slowly, steadily shoved the Buick sideways into the thicket.

All we could see from the cab was the roof of the Buick just past the Jimmy's hood. As the car slid and scraped along, the roof flexed and twisted in the spotlights. Beyond the roof, the tops of bushes quivered and dropped out of sight as the car was pushed over them.

Finally, the Buick jammed solid against the larger trees in the thicket. Cowboy backed the Jimmy up a short distance to light up the scene, and we bailed out.

Cowboy went wide to the left, staying in the shadows. I tucked in close to the Jimmy's front fender. The side of the Buick looked like rumpled maroon corduroy.

"Hey, you guys," I called, "can Elmo come out and play?"

". . . the hell's going on here, hoss?" Nagle's indignant voice got louder and louder as he picked himself off the floor of the Buick. He peered cautiously out the hole where the rear side window used to be. His caterpillar eyebrows looked like a gray McDonald's sign for an instant, then he ducked out of sight.

Cowboy bulled his way through the bushes toward the front of the Buick. When he got there, he used the hood as a bench rest for his shotgun. He nodded once.

"Okay, gentlemen," I called. "Party's over. I'll have the weapons first. Hold 'em by the barrels and drop 'em out the windows."

There was an inarticulate shout from the Buick. A shape

rose in the front seat, and a handful of black revolver poked out the window. The pistol went off with a flat crack. One of the Jimmy's spotlights went out. Not bad shooting, even that close.

Cowboy let off one round from his shotgun.

The hand and pistol quivered in a red haze for a quarter second; then the pistol jerked and spun to the ground. The arm and what was left of the hand retracted into the Buick.

There were sounds, too. There was the loud but dull boom of Cowboy's twelve gauge, a surprisingly high-pitched scream from inside the Buick, and soft pings as a few pellets ricocheted off the pistol and pattered onto the front of the Jimmy.

Eight seconds later, two handguns were gingerly lowered out the windows. After that, they held up five empty hands where we could see them. All five hands were whole and unscarred. I didn't insist on seeing the sixth. Why get bogged down with petty details?

I said, "Come out of the car one at a time. Backward. Any faces I see will end up looking like The Hero's hand."

Nagle sent the goons out first. Cowboy frisked them, then draped them facedown over the Buick. The Hero was white-faced and shaking; his hand looked terrible, the dumb bastard. Cowboy rigged a tourniquet with Hero's belt and let him lay on the hood with his bad arm raised against the windshield. The other goon he put on the wavy car roof.

Nagle finally came out, upset but trying to act unconcerned. He squinted against the lights. After Cowboy had patted him down, I let Nagle see me.

"Ah, well, I get it now, hoss. Thought you old boys was Martello's at first. Glad you're not." He smiled broadly. Good old Uncle Elmo. "I guess you got away from those apartment house folks okay."

"I'll check the car," I said to Cowboy.

The video was in a white plastic shopping bag on the glass-littered back seat. It looked like the same one, but I couldn't be sure, so I searched the rest of the car. There were no more tapes, but when I ripped the rear seat out, I found an oily MAC-10, a noise suppressor, and two empty clips, all wrapped up in an old bed sheet.

I waved the chunky little submachine gun at Nagle. "Kind of overconfident, weren't you? If you'd had this thing in action instead of storage, you might have had a chance."

Nagle didn't look very happy; he probably thought the same thing.

Cowboy said, "Mimi loves them little chatterboxes. Is that a nine millimeter?"

"Nope. Looks like a .45 to me."

"Damn," Cowboy said. "A .45's too much gun for Mimi."

"It's too much gun for Happy Elmo here, too," I said. "We'll dump it in the lake later."

Nagle looked even less happy.

"Listen up, Nagle," I said. "If this isn't the right video, we'll be back. And you can erase any copies, because Hadley won't be paying off."

"Say, hoss," he said with a smile that seemed to take a lot of work, "we kinda got off on the wrong foot right from the beginning. No need for that. Hey, if I'd known ole Hadley had hired two of us, why, I wouldn't have taken that video away from you. We could have worked together. Hell, we still can."

He nodded his round, happy head at the plastic gadget in my hand. "That's worth ten thousand dollars to you, old hoss. Think about it."

"You get in my way again, Nagle, and I'll blow one of *your* hands off," I said. "Think about that."

Cowboy said, "Long as we're thinkin' about all this stuff, you want to think about getting out of here?"

"Why not? Somebody might have heard those shots."

"Oh, it ain't that," Cowboy said. "But we don't want to run late for our next appointment. Folks might get nervous."

When we last saw him, Nagle was still standing beside the battered Buick. His two leg breakers clumsily crawled off the car. Then Cowboy backed the Jimmy out of the brush and onto the road, we switched off the fancy light show, and drove away.

"Not bad," I said. "That's Step One out of the way."

Cowboy grunted as he wheeled the Jimmy around a tight

curve, "You must be lookin' forward to Step Two. You grinnin' like a mule eating sweetbriers."

"True," I said cheerfully. "I just love to double-cross people like Walter Hadley."

CHAPTER TWENTY-ONE

Hadley's pretty company car was parked in the shadows off Garland Road, near the White Rock Lake spillway. Hadley paced up and down beside the car. He jumped, startled, when I pulled in and got out of the Mustang.

He ran toward me. "What happened? Is it over? Where's . . . I mean, no one got hurt, did they?"

"Cowboy's dumping the truck," I said to Mimi. "He'll be right along."

Mimi grinned. "You two old poops pulled off another one, did you?" Mimi sat on the fender of Hadley's Olds and slowly banged her boot heels together. Her boots were a long way from the ground, and when I stood beside her, the crown of her Western hat was a good six inches below my eye-level.

Let's face it, Mimi was short.

She'd once been called a midget, but the biker who said that was just angry because Mimi shot him. Mimi wasn't a midget, but she was very short. And cute, too. She always reminded me of a Kewpie doll in cowboy clothes.

Hadley tugged at my shirtsleeve like a little kid. "A police car stopped," he said. "About forty-five minutes ago." He pointed furtively at Mimi and lowered his voice. "She pretended we were parked here. You know, *parked* here."

"That was the whole idea. The cops went away, didn't they?"

"Yes," Hadley said, nodding jerkily. "But they looked at me strangely. She's so *young*."

Mimi hooted cheerfully. "Don't I wish, honey. Don't I wish."

I said, "Oh, for Christ's sake, Wally. Settle down. Mimi's older than Cricket was, and you act like she was jailbait. Besides, what do you care what a couple of bored patrol cops think?"

"She is? But . . ."

Cowboy's pickup pulled in and parked. He ambled lazily over and leaned against the Olds next to Mimi. She wrinkled her nose at him and bumped her shoulder against his. Cowboy smiled placidly.

"Okay, Wally," I said, "we got the video away from that bad, bad man who doesn't like you. Now let's talk about expenses."

Hadley's eyes narrowed. "You *are* going to try the same thing—"

"No, I'm not! This is a freebie as far as I'm concerned. I said I'd do it, and I did. But I had to bring in help, and it's only fair that you pay those expenses. Cowboy, what are you charging me for tonight?"

Cowboy looked at Mimi, who shrugged. He shrugged, too, and said, "Aw, call it three hundred."

I snapped my fingers at Hadley and jerked my thumb toward Cowboy. Hadley bitched and moaned for a minute or two, then he dug out his wallet and counted fifties into Cowboy's palm.

Then Hadley turned and held out his hand imperiously. "The video," he said.

"Oh, didn't I mention that part?" I said. "You can't have it yet."

Mike Norbuck waved wearily at the big black man with the Uzi. "It's okay, it's okay," he said.

The guard backed off slowly, glaring at me with obvious distrust. He was big, that guy. Six six, anyway, which gave him a good four inches over me. And about twenty pounds, I'd guess. Plus the Uzi.

As I sidled past him in the narrow hallway, I realized he looked like Avery Brooks. I wondered if he could say "Spensah!" like Avery Brooks did. I'd have asked him, but he was busy and it was pretty late and what the hell. . . .

"Thanks, Mike," I said to Norbuck. "This is a big help to me."

There were several places in Dallas where you could have copies made of the video from your kid's birthday party or your niece's wedding. But those places weren't open at this hour of the morning. And, even if they had been, they tended to get a little tight around the jawline when asked to copy the kind of video I had.

Or thought I had. It suddenly came to me that I wasn't sure I even had the right one. And that I'd never seen the full Cricket-Hadley video, anyway.

I never used to think of things like that fifteen years ago.

In any case, if you had the kind of video I thought I had and if you knew where Mike Norbuck operated his specialized copying service, then you, too, might have found yourself walking through Mike's door at 1:30 A.M., hoping the guy with the Uzi had already killed his quota for the day. So he'd be mellowed down and amiable.

"Come on through," Mike said. He led me to a back room where shiny machines whirred and burped. A skinny kid with glasses fed tapes to the machines and pushed buttons. A shotgun leaned against the wall.

Mike had one of those businesses you don't find in the Yellow Pages. He copied porno videos in bulk for certain mail order dealers. He charged a lot of money for that service. Which meant some of the porn dealers occasionally tried to cut their costs by hijacking Mike's output before it went to the rightful owners.

Copying porno videos was you might call a stressful occupation.

"I kept a slot open for you," Mike said. "You sure you only want the one copy?"

"Uh-huh. It's a personal matter, not sale stock."

Mike nodded without expression. Mike did almost everything without expression. He had a broad, flat face, hooded eyes, and narrow lips that barely moved when he spoke. He was the only person I ever knew who could laugh without having the corners of his mouth turn up.

I said, "Uh, could we check it first? I just, um, came by this. I think it's the right one, but . . ."

Mike did electronic-y things with my video. A television screen lit up with the picture of Walter Hadley sitting on Cricket's couch.

Mike looked at me. His eyebrows were raised a quarter of an inch, which was Mike's way of screaming to be answered.

"That's it," I said.

He looked at the screen critically and adjusted controls. "Lousy picture quality," he said, "and it's silent. Amateur?"

"Yeah. Kind of a nostalgia film. The male lead wears a mask and leaves his socks on."

Mike sniffed. He turned off the TV monitor and began recording Hadley's evening of passion onto an old video cassette labeled "Teenage Lust Kittens."

"You're sure there's no sound at all on there, Mike? I'd like to hear it, no matter how weak or scratchy it is."

Mike ran a red-handled control to the end of its travel, cocked his head, then shrugged. "There you are. Deader than a wedge."

When the machines burped, Mike gave me both tapes. I tried to give him a fifty, but he waved it away.

"Naw," he said, "forget it. What with the money you got back for me last year, I can afford one lousy dub."

Hey, I never claimed my clients were all philosophers and archbishops.

Mike walked me out to the Mustang. On the way, he touted a film investment opportunity. "It can't miss," he said. "I'm in for five percent of the deal. I can get you in, too, if you want." He told me about the planned movie.

I told him a porno version of "Gilligan's Island" sounded surefire, but I couldn't afford it right then.

Mike shrugged. "Well," he said, "that's show business."

Hadley had waited in his car, fuming under the flat, hard stare of Mike's outside guard. I handed Hadley the original video, and he drove away without a word.

"You're welcome," I snarled at his receding taillights. Then I thanked Mike again, said good-bye, and drove to Hilda's house.

It was almost 3:00 A.M. when I crawled into bed. Hilda was asleep. She jumped when my foot bumped her leg, then she relaxed and squirmed over to my side of the bed.

"Es muy hombre," she muttered sleepily. We'd been dredging up forgotten high school Spanish before I'd left earlier that evening. Hilda thought it would be fun to go through the entire San Antonio weekend without speaking English.

I didn't think I could make it. Right then, for example, I fell asleep before I could work out how to say "stick 'em up" in Spanish.

CHAPTER TWENTY-TWO

"Come on, Rafferty. We'll miss the plane." Hilda stood beside her BMW and fidgeted.

I shoved my copy of the Hadley-Dawes video into my pocket. Then I took it out and put it into the Mustang glove compartment. Then I put it back into my pocket.

I didn't like the idea of leaving it lying around where someone—Nagle, Hadley, Winchester, who?—could swipe it, and I thought the airline security scanners might erase it.

Carry it with me? What if that stupid walk-through gadget beeped because I had too much change in my pocket? No one wants to get searched when they're carrying a video labeled "Teenage Lust Kittens."

Hilda honked the horn. I left the video in the Mustang.

Good move. The walk-through gadget did beep. Hilda didn't understand why that was so funny.

In San Antonio, we stayed at the Palacio del Rio, in a room with a balcony overlooking the River Walk. Love that River Walk. Where else could you wander along two miles of river parkland in the middle of downtown?

We did all the things tourists do in San Antonio. We ate and drank and people-watched from an outside table at the Little Rhein Steakhouse. We strolled through La Villita, told each other we'd shop sensibly and didn't. Well, Hilda didn't. I did. I could wear a *guayabera* shirt lots of places. Really.

We went through HemisFair Plaza, too, and up the Tower of the Americas, and we looked at the old missions.

And we went to the Alamo. Again.

"How many times have you been here?" Hilda said. It was hot and a little sticky in the courtyard outside the chapel building. There were shade trees, but the walls stopped the breeze.

"This is my fourth time," I said. "It kind of grows on you."

Hilda shuddered. "Don't you think it's gruesome, though? I mean, we might be standing on an unmarked grave right now."

"There weren't any graves, babe. The Mexican troops burned the bodies, then scraped the ashes into a hole in the ground."

A Hispanic couple with a small child walked past us. The little girl had a lollipop and big dark eyes. I smiled at her; she goggled at me.

Hilda waited until they were out of earshot and said, "But all this Remember-the-Alamo stuff is just an excuse for racism, isn't it?"

"I don't know. If it is, that came later. It had nothing to do with these men. This was political; this was a freedom fight or a revolution, take your pick, but it was not racist. Example: only six of the men who died defending this place had been born in Texas. And all six were Mexican. Well, Hispanic, anyway."

Hilda frowned at that. She turned, slowly, in a complete circle. When she faced me again, she had a confused look on her face.

The Alamo had bothered me the first time, too. It was smaller and shabbier than I'd expected; hardly worth fighting for. And the location was disconcerting. The main entrance, with its adobe arch and heavy wooden door, looked across a wide street at part of downtown San Antonio.

Hilda said, "I know it's historic and all, but it's kind of tacky, too. How about that old movie poster in there with John Wayne and Richard Widmark? They're milking this place for all it's worth. Why let it get to you?"

"Something happened here that's important, Hil, but I don't fully understand it." I sighed and looked at the inside of the wall. I tried to imagine three thousand combat troops on the other side.

"Early one morning in 1836," I said, "one hundred and eighty-two men died here. They were outnumbered fifteen to one; they had known for two weeks they couldn't defend this place. And they knew there would be no prisoners taken. It was win or die, and they couldn't win. So why did they stay?"

"Where could they go? They were surrounded, weren't they?"

"In the beginning, Santa Anna offered to let them walk away, if they would abandon the mission. And even later, they probably could have slipped out through the Mexican lines. Thirty volunteers sneaked in after the siege started. And Jim Bonham got out twice. He came back both times."

I kicked dust with one foot and watched it settle. "They could have quit, babe. It would have been embarrassing, especially for men like Crockett and Bowie and Travis, but they could have quit."

"Pride?" Hilda said softly.

"Maybe," I said. "Maybe they stayed because they were proud. Or brave. Or stupid. I don't know why they stayed, Hil. I wish I did."

"Men!" Hilda's tone was sharp, angry. She wouldn't look at me as she said, "What about you, Rafferty? Would you have stayed?"

I took her hand and squeezed it. She did not squeeze back. I said, "I don't know, babe. I honestly do not know. Maybe that's why this place fascinates me so much."

"It doesn't fascinate me," Hilda said. "I hate it."

Then she did squeeze my hand. Hard, with her fingernails digging into my flesh.

"I hate it because I know you, Rafferty. You'd have stayed. Goddamn it, you'd have stayed."

CHAPTER TWENTY-THREE

Saturday afternoon Hilda went shopping. Serious shopping, she called it. No-holds-barred, professional shopping, I called it, where only the strong survived and mere males were left behind where they fell.

Hilda thought about it, then decided that was an entirely reasonable description.

I sat around the coffee shop awhile, then went up to the room and phoned Dallas. I was feeling vaguely guilty about taking a weekend off in the middle of a case. Or maybe I was turning into a closet workaholic. What was next? Not—horror of horrors—yuppiedom?

The voice on duty at my answering service sounded impressed; five messages was way over my quota. I scribbled down the names, thanked the voice, and sat wondering at my newly acquired desirability.

Walter Hadley wanted me to call him back. I tried to think of what Hadley could say that I wanted to hear. Apology? Thank-you? Come to my barbecue on Sunday? Forget it, Wally. I scratched heavy lines through his name.

My environmental expert, The Grape, had called. He left a number I didn't recognize; his home, maybe. Wherever it was, no one answered the phone.

The next name was Sergeant Ricco, Dallas Police Department. Ricco's message was simple: *Come see us.* The unwritten message went on from there: *. . . or we'll come get you*. I assumed Ricco and Ed Durkee had a few hundred pointed questions about me, Nagle, totaled Buicks, and shotguns in the park.

I tried. It wasn't my fault Ricco was off duty. I left a message promising to show up by Monday afternoon at the very latest. As I hung up, I began practicing my lines for the opening performance of *Who, Me?*, a Rafferty Extravaganza and One-Man Show Guaranteed to Amuse and Delight.

It would not be my first appearance in the role.

There were two messages from the Green Army contingent. According to my list, Linda Taree's call had come in first. She had left a message—"What's new?"—but no telephone number, which greatly simplified my branch-office paperwork. Sccrrratch.

Winchester was next. He had left a number, so I didn't have a ready excuse not to phone him. I scratched his name out anyway, then thought about it and wrote him back in. After all, I was working for him. At least, I was using his money. And I'd used up all he'd given me so far. It was time to go back to the well.

The net result of all that industry was more work; I had a hot date with two suspicious cops, and I still had to find The Grape. I tried his number again. Still no answer.

Hilda came back to the room about five-thirty with an armload of clothing boxes. She modeled everything for me, which was fun. I told her none of her stuff was as practical as my *guayabera* shirt.

"Ho, ho," she said. "Even if that was true—which it isn't—my stuff is much sexier."

"Ho, ho, yourself. Watch this." I took off all my clothes, then modeled the *guayabera* for her. She countered with a selection of new lingerie.

What with all that sophisticated fashion modeling and, well, other diversions, we decided to stay in and have a roomservice meal that evening. When it came, Hilda hid in the bathroom. I wrapped a bath towel around my waist. It seemed to be an occasion where I needed something more than just an ornate Mexican shirt.

I thought I looked casually elegant, but the Hispanic room service waiter seemed to have difficulty suppressing a laugh. After he'd laid out the meal and presented the bill, I struck a pose and said, "Olé!"

He grinned and murmured, "Loco turista," but he didn't say that very loudly, and he didn't say it at all until after he had the tip in his hand.

At three in the morning I was out on the balcony, leaning on my elbows, idly watching the River Walk four stories below. A couple, arm in arm, disappeared around a bend to my left. After a few minutes two finger-popping, chattering teenage boys diddly-bopped into view from the right.

The River Walk never stopped; the pulse merely slowed periodically.

I was deep in thought when Hilda whispered, "Hey, Ugly," and pressed herself against my back. She wore a thin silk robe, a trophy of the shopping expedition, and her body was warm through it.

"Umm, you feel good," she said. "How'd you like to escort me to St. Louis next week, hunk?"

"You women are such animals."

"Well, you stand out here with no clothes on, big guy, you're bound to get offers."

"Yeah," I said. "You're the second tonight, as it happens. The chairperson of the South San Antonio Radical Feminist's Action Brigade stopped by. She wanted to become my love slave."

"Uh-huh," Hilda said. "That's a rather unusual attitude for a militant feminist, I would think."

"Oh, she offered to recant. Said she would buy a bra, wear makeup, learn to cook, all that stuff."

Hilda jabbed a thumbnail into my side and twisted it back and forth. Good thing I'm so tough. Otherwise, that would have hurt like hell.

Hilda said, "Be serious, you nut. What's the matter? Can't sleep?"

I shook my head. "I woke up and got to thinking about

the Dawes case. It's funny, babe. Most cases have one or two people who don't quite add up, but I can't remember another one where *no one* added up.''

Hilda came around and leaned one elbow on the balcony railing. A light on the River Walk outlined her body beneath the thin robe. ''I thought you had everyone figured out,'' she said.

''I did, too, once. But now . . . Here, follow me through this mess. Cricket Dawes got the brush-off from her married boyfriend. And she took it hard. Okay, she might have been a little more serious than Hadley about their romance, but even so, why try to smear a big company? And why bring in The Green Army? She had never shown any interest in that sort of thing before. You see, Hil, it makes sense, sort of, but it seems both overly complicated and heavy-handed; like killing ants with remote control sledge hammers.

''Next: Hadley, the boyfriend. It's possible he confronted Cricket about the files—or the video—and they argued. Maybe he belted her a good one, she fell down, and died. Maybe, but I have trouble with that. Hadley's a wimp; he doesn't do anything himself. He hired Nagle to recover the video. He brought in company muscle to threaten me. He let me take the video away from Nagle. And he whined like a little kid until I set up Mimi to baby-sit with him that night.''

I was building up a fair head of steam, expounding theories to the night air. Hilda listened quietly. The light behind her hair made the curly edges glow. Her eyes were small bright stars in the shadow on her face.

''Winchester,'' I continued. ''Well, he comes the closest to making sense. He's a two-faced bastard, but I think I can see both sides of the street he's working.

''Linda. The redhead. She comes on to me, then she's ready to scoop my eyes out like melon balls. Then she camps on my doorstep, comes on to me again, and—when I respectfully decline her experienced services—she wants to ''keep in touch'' because of her abiding interest in the Dawes matter. Figure that one out.

''That's the whole problem, babe. They're *all* squirrelly. I can't tell the good guys from the bad guys without a program, and so far there's nobody walking through the bleachers selling programs.''

''Does it really matter?'' Hilda said. ''I thought your plan is to show who did *not* kill that woman, which would mean a mugger must have done it, and then you'll have accomplished what you wanted, no matter how squirrelly these people are.'' She bit her lip thoughtfully. ''Did I get that right?''

''Yeah, that's right,'' I said. ''That's the plan.''

I put my arm around her and we watched the lights for a while, then went back to bed.

I didn't sleep for a long time, though, and the Dawes case was still bugging me the next day when we shuffled into the big tin bird.

All the way back to Dallas, uniformed women wearing too much makeup smiled relentlessly at us.

Maybe they were just trying to cheer me up.

CHAPTER TWENTY-FOUR

"Hey, Rafferty, don't misunderstand me," Ricco said. "Anybody who fucks over Elmo Nagle, they're okay in my book." Ricco smiled at me. The smile made him look like a manic weasel.

"I wish I could help you guys," I said. "I really do, but . . ." I held my hands outspread at shoulder height to indicate my honesty and willingness to cooperate. I smiled, too. That combination gets 'em every time.

Ed Durkee rubbed a big hand over his rubbery jowls. "Rafferty," he said slowly, "you're full of shit."

Well, most times it gets 'em.

"Look," I said, "I shouldn't have to tell you guys this, but you've got your roles mixed up. Ricco, you should be the bad cop. Ed, you should be the good cop. Try it that way. You'll see, I'll confess to something. Promise."

Ed slurped coffee from his mug. He looked tired, though Ed had one of those faces that always looked tired.

"Let me get this straight," he said. "You're telling me that you called Ricco to ask for information about Nagle, but you don't know anything about what happened to Nagle's car the next night?"

"Bingo. And, hey, you guys have me all atwitter with curiosity here. What did happen to Nagle's car?"

Ricco kicked a chair over. "I'll twitter you, Rafferty, you—"

"Shut up, Ricco," Ed said. He looked at him blandly until Ricco picked up the chair and sat in it. Ed continued to look at him and said, "Rafferty's right, though. You are better as the bad cop."

Ed turned to me and calmly told me that Nagle's Buick had been found. He referred to it as "damaged." He admitted there were no witnesses; an anonymous caller had reported hearing gunshots an hour earlier. Ed's theory involved parked teenage lovers and a belated sense of civic responsibility.

It was all interesting stuff, but the most interesting parts were those he left out. Ed didn't mention Nagle; he didn't mention a wounded goon, and he somehow made a big mistake about the location. Silly Ed.

"Well, in the first place," I said, "I haven't been near Lake Ray Hubbard since . . . hell, I don't know when. That's way out past Garland, Ed."

He said, "Yeah."

I said, "I suppose you think this Nagle jerk and I had a fender bender. While sightseeing. At Lake Ray Hubbard."

Ricco snorted. "Fender bender, my ass. Goddamn car looks like a tank ran over it."

I let Ed look into my wide blue eyes. "What is he talking about, pray tell?"

"Cute," Ed said, "very cute." He sighed. "Something big and heavy pushed Nagle's car so far into a bunch of scrub it took a wrecker to get it out."

"Well, it wasn't my Mustang," I said.

"I know that rust-bucket you drive couldn't do that," Ed said. "There were a couple of trucks stolen that night, though, and one of them could have. When we find . . ."

"Ed, I love it when you let your voice trail off like that. It's powerful. Menacing. Hey, have you ever thought about doing any radio work? Try saying, 'The tree of evil bears bitter—' "

Ed held up one big palm in a *stop* gesture. I stopped. Maybe I was laying it on a little thick.

"Okay, Ed, I'll settle down," I said. "But how about you knock off the crap, too, eh?"

"Crap?" He mustered up an indignant look. "You're the one in the crap. Nagle's statement mentioned you. You're gone this time, Rafferty."

I held out my wrists. "Okay, copper, ya got me. Slap da cuffs on and take me to da big house."

We looked at each other for a minute, perhaps two. Then Ed waved at the air between us. "Okay, okay." He rolled his eyes. "When are you going to grow up?"

Ricco sniffed disdainfully and refused to look at either of us.

I said, "Rafferty's Rule Number Twenty-one: Grow up and grow old. Think about that, Ed."

"This may be just a game of grab-ass to you, Rafferty, but I'm not laughing. Nagle's got some song-and-dance about how his car was stolen, and he doesn't know why it got wrecked at White Rock—"

I drew breath to score a point about Ed's deliberate Lake Ray Hubbard–White Rock Lake mix up. Then I saw the look in his eyes and decided not to interrupt.

". . . Lake," Ed said, and silently dared me to make something of it. After two long beats, he went on. "So Nagle's no help. And you, being your usual smart-ass self, are even less use to me. But you're not fooling anybody, goddamn it! What do you think, we're all asleep down here? We know you and Nagle tangled last Thursday night about something. My guess is Nagle had two or three of his mouth-breathers with him. And you probably had that hayseed gun-slinger Cowboy on your side."

Ed shook his big head wearily. "Christ! When I think about you jerks out there playing dodgem cars and letting off rounds at each other . . ."

Ricco chimed in with, "You're fucking crazy, Rafferty. You can't get away with that private-war shit." Ricco's indignation was less than convincing; he sounded like he was miffed because he hadn't been invited.

Ed grimaced at me, pawed aimlessly through the papers on his desk, and finally said, "I'm serious about this, Rafferty. If you have anything on Nagle, let's have it. There are a couple of people in the department trying to put that bastard away.''

"I don't have anything, Ed. His name came up on the sidelines of a case. I checked him out with Ricco. That's it. That's all. Finito. Don't make a meal of it, for God's sake.''

Okay, so I lied to Ed. So what? The only thing I had on Nagle was the Hadley blackmail, and Hadley would never admit it had ever happened.

Ed didn't quite buy it, but there wasn't much he could do except glare at me suspiciously. He did so.

"And," I said, "if I accidentally stumble over anything involving Nagle, I promise to bring it to you immediately. I will expect a community service award, of course, presented at a tasteful ceremony. By a deputy chief, at least. And we should invite—''

"Rafferty!" Ed boomed, "get outta here!''

So much for the professional courtesies; now I could go back to work.

CHAPTER TWENTY-FIVE

After leaving the cop shop, I carted sandwiches and beer to the office. Rafferty's power lunch.

I tried the number The Grape had left with my service, lo these many days. Still no answer. Then I looked up The Grape's home phone in the book, and the numbers matched. How's that for sleuth-ery?

It seemed reasonable that Grape wouldn't be home at noon on a Monday, so I tried his office. The Grape's receptionist would not admit he was there—you could flunk out of Famous Receptionist School for that—and she launched into the old "I'll-see-if-he's-free" routine with a straight face. Well, a straight voice.

"And whom shall I say is calling?" It was Gail; we'd engaged in mock battle before; I was running out of routines.

"Jeremy Farthinggill-Humboldt," I said in what I call my English accent. "Recording Secretary, Land Rights for Gay Whales Committee."

"Weak, Rafferty, weak," Gail said. "About a six and a half, I'd say. Hang on."

While I was waiting, my office door opened. Linda Taree stuck her head into the room.

The Grape clicked onto the line with, "Oh, damn, I hope you didn't try my home number all weekend."

"Oh, damn, I hope it's not too late for whatever you called

me about.'' I waved the skinny redhead in and pointed to a chair.

''No,'' The Grape said, ''we're okay for time. I found the guy for what you want.''

Linda sat in the plastic chair and smiled hello.

''Uh, Grape, what exactly are you . . . ?''

It was a little disconcerting to have Linda there while I talked to The Grape. This case was screwy enough without having people from one end of it listening while I talked to people from the—

''Trust me,'' Grape said.''This guy is perfect.''

''Oh, I get it now. The expert.''

''Right. This guy knows all about reprocessing nuclear fuel. Not only that, but he worked for Dormac-Chaffee, at the plant we all know and love to hate. He was a lab technician there until about, oh, I forget exactly, six or eight months ago. How about them apples?''

''Wonderful,'' I said. ''I owe you, Grape. Gimme his name and number.''

''No,'' The Grape said, ''he won't play that way. Look, he's using the name George. He'll phone you tonight. You two can work out a safe place to meet.''

It sounded like The Grape and his buddy had come down with Winchester's disease. *Using the name? A safe place to meet?*

''Hey, time out, Grape,'' I said. ''How straight is this clown? I am suspicious of people who use phony names and want to meet in parking lots at midnight.''

''He's got his reasons. He had complained a lot about how Dormac-Chaffee did things. When he finally quit, they dumped on him. It took him four months to find another lab job, and he's pretty goosey now. He'll talk about what goes on out there, but he's got a family. He's being careful, that's all.''

''Uh-huh,'' I said. I stole a look at Linda. She was glancing around my office, pretending she was ignoring what I said, like we all do in that situation.

''He'll phone you tonight between six and seven,'' Grape said. ''I gave him your office number.''

"I'll be here," I said, "and speaking of numbers, where the hell were you all weekend?"

The Grape said, "Funny thing, that. I left my home number with your service last thing Friday afternoon. Well, I stopped for a drink on the way home, and I got to talking with the drink waitress. About ecology and the environment and all. Before I knew it, her shift was over and we went to her place for a meal and . . . next time I looked around, the weekend was gone. You know how it is." He chuckled fondly.

"Aw, bullshit," I said. "No vegetarian could do that. Not for a whole weekend. Not on wheat germ and bean sprouts."

Grape chuckled again.

"Well, maybe," I said, "if you took frequent rest breaks and avoided sexy pillow talk about long-line fishing and re-planting pine forests."

"Rafferty, there are some things a gentleman never tells." Grape chuckled a third time; an especially knowing and satisfied chuckle. "Don't forget, George will call you between six and seven tonight."

He was still chuckling when he hung up.

When I hung up, too, Linda Taree turned brightly toward me and said, "I'm not interrupting anything, am I?"

"Only lunch, and there's plenty of that." I pushed a corned-beef-on-rye toward her. She refused the sandwich, but accepted my last beer. Damn!

We ate and drank without talking for a while, then she finally said, "Well, what's new?"

"Not much," I mumbled around a mouthful.

No apologies for the less-than-scintillating repartee. I was thinking about the Hadley-Dawes video in my desk drawer. If they had talked shop before they jumped into the sack, maybe I ought to "listen" to that tape before I met The Grape's snitch. But to do that, I needed a . . .

"Hey," I said to Linda Taree, "how would you like to thrill to the adventure and excitement of modern private detection?"

"What?" she said. "Help you with this job, uh, case, whatever you call it?"

"Yep," I said. "Find me a person who reads lips."

She gave me a skeptical look.

I took the video out of the drawer and held it up.

"Oh, terrific," Linda said sourly. " 'Teenage Lust—' "

"Never mind the label, dammit. It's been copied over. Cricket Dawes and her boyfriend made it as a turn-on. The first few minutes show them chatting over drinks before the boyfriend knew the recorder was on. I want to know what they said. Problem is, the tape has no audio track. But I figure someone like you should know a person who can . . ."

What was it with this woman? Usually, I could go for months without inadvertently insulting a feminist. With Linda Taree, every time I opened my mouth I messed up. Maybe I was trying too hard.

I waffled on, gulping shoe leather with every word. "Well, I mean, you're interested in these community service–type things and helping people and all that sort of—"

"Oh, shut up," Linda said. "You're only making it worse. But, okay, I get the idea. I think I can find someone. When do you want to do it?"

"As soon as possible," I said. "You find a lip-reader, I'll get a VCR in here."

She nodded, brow crinkled in thought. "Let me use your phone."

She called three different places and asked for "Billy" each time. The third time, she made contact, explained the job, and hung up with a satisifed smile.

"Billy needs a ride," she said. "We'll meet you back here in an hour, okay?"

"Great."

Billy; that was good. When the tape got raunchy, Linda could wait in the hallway while Bill and I checked to see if they said anything after the sex.

Linda left. So did I, headed for the nearest TV rental place with a spring in my step.

Exactly sixty-three minutes later, my spring uncoiled. Linda came back to the office without good old Bill. Or even Billy.

Instead, she waltzed in with Billie.

Billie was braless under a Huey Lewis T-shirt. Billie had braces on her teeth.

And Billie looked fifteen years old. Sixteen, tops.

CHAPTER TWENTY-SIX

"Wait a minute," I said, "wait just one minute here."

Linda grinned wolfishly. Billie—I found myself thinking of her as Billie the Kid—slumped into a hip-shot stance and curled her lip. Or maybe her lip had snagged on her tin grin.

"Damn it, Linda," I said, "I told you what's on this tape! What's the big idea dragging a sixth-grader in here—"

They both broke up laughing. Billie the Kid pawed through a huge raggedy shoulder bag and came up with a wallet. She handed it to me.

Son-of-a-gun. Billie Kentoff was twenty-two years old. She had a driver's license and credit cards to prove it. She also had a smart mouth.

"Happy now, old-timer?"

"Well . . . okay," I said. "Uh, thanks for your help."

"Sure," she said, and she laughed. So did Linda Taree.

When I had set up the rented TV and VCR, I'd arranged them so the screen faced away from the window between my office and Honeybutt's. Honeybutt had been giving me strange looks ever since the scuffle with Hadley and his security goons; I could imagine what she would think if she saw me watching porno videos with a pair like Linda and Billie. Honeybutt might never wink at me again. Or file anything in the bottom drawer.

"All right, then," I said to Billie. "I'll show you the part I'm interested in. There are—"

"Take it easy, hotshot," Billie said. She plunked herself down in front of the video gear and dug a notepad out of her bag. A pencil had been stuck into the wire binding of the pad. She pulled it free and pointed it at me. "Now look," she said briskly, "I don't have all day for this, so let's just get to work, okay? Where do you start this thing?"

It was very strange listening to her. Billie's voice was tough-cookie street-smart, but her appearance was aw-Mom-why-not?-All-the-other-kids-are-allowed-to.

Maybe there was something to that generation-gap business, after all.

Billie peered at the controls of the VCR, stabbed a button, and the TV screen began to flicker and twitch.

I cleared my throat. "Er, after five or six minutes, it gets a little—"

"Relax, Pop, I've seen people fuck before." She rolled her eyes at Linda. "Shit," she muttered, "what does he think this is, 1975 or something?"

Pop? 1975 as the Dark Ages?

Even for a Monday, the day was shaping up as bad news.

The TV screen burped silently and showed us Walter Hadley sitting on Cricket's sofa. Billie watched closely, her eyes never leaving the screen while her right hand made notes in Gregg's finest scrawl. Linda scootched her chair closer.

I sighed and looked through the window at Honeybutt. She looked up curiously, and I winked at her. She winked back, but I could tell her heart wasn't in it.

Billie ran the tape all the way through. I watched the part I had missed when Nagle hijacked the video that embarrassing night in Cricket's apartment.

As it turned out, I hadn't missed anything of, well, professional interest.

There were long moments of empty bed, then Cricket rolled into view with a wickedly funny grin on her face. Hadley came more tentatively to video stardom. He kept his face turned away from the camera at first, but Cricket tickled him and jollied him along. Eventually they made love, got it on, screwed their brains out, depending on your vintage and attitude about such things.

I found watching the tape somewhat depressing, mostly, I think, because I knew what had happened to Cricket Dawes since then.

Billie and Linda weren't the kind to dwell on such niceties. When the tape ended, Billie punched the rewind button and leaned back in her chair. "Well, there's one we lost," she said to Linda. "Did you see how she played up to that pig? Gross!"

"Yes. And notice the bikini-line bush? Wax job, you think?"

"Could be." Billie shuddered. "How could anyone do that?" She turned to me. "Hey, macho man, would you smear wax on your chest, then rip out all the hair just because I said it would look sexy?"

I shook my head.

Billie turned back to Linda with a Fonzie-like "ehhhhhh!"

Billie watched the video again, following along in her notes as she did so. I didn't watch that time; I turned around to stare at Honeybutt pounding her typewriter in the next office. It wasn't too exciting, but it was dependable.

After the second time through, while the tape was rewinding again, Billie and Linda chatted about Billie's job. It seemed she worked for some government agency, teaching deaf children to lip-read. A little boy named Quentin was doing especially well.

Billie ran the video a third time. At one point she clacked buttons in a slow, regular cadence, running a short segment of the tape again and again. As she did so, she silently mouthed a phrase. Finally she nodded to herself, made a correction on her notes and let the tape run on.

Then I realized Honeybutt had stopped typing. She was sitting oddly, too, leaning to one side and staring up into my office. Not at me, though, or at Billie or at Linda, but at something on the wall. She had an unusual look on her face, too: surprised, but with a small, privately amused smile.

I got up and went to the window. Honeybutt started

abruptly and began to type furiously. She kept her face down and her eyes on the typewriter.

When I bent down and looked along her line of sight, I saw why. The TV screen was reflected in a glass-covered print on my office wall. Superimposed on the print with surprisingly good picture quality, Walter and Cricket, er, disported themselves immodestly.

After that I stood in front of the window until Billie finished her work and turned off the video gadgetry.

"Okay," Billie said, riffling back to the beginning of her notes. "I got maybe sixty percent of their conversation. You want me to read this?"

"Wait a minute." I used my little tape recorder; I couldn't read shorthand, and taking notes of notes seemed like overkill.

"Well, first off," Billie said, "he's Wally-bear and she's Cricky or Creeky. Sometimes it looks like one; sometimes the other."

"Cricky, probably. Her nickname's Cricket."

Billie made a careful adjustment to her notes. Then she read Walter and Cricket's four-month-old conversation into my tape recorder.

There were two important parts to that conversation. I understood one part very well; Wally-bear was an even bigger louse than I'd thought.

When Hadley had spilled his guts to me in his fancy company car, he made his relationship with Cricket sound like the fabled "brief, meaningless affair." On the tape, though, Wally knit his distinguished brows and fed Cricket a crock about waiting until "Jenny finishes middle school before I file for the divorce."

Billie paused there and sneered. Her braces made the sneer looked vaguely robotic. She said to me, "Is this asshole a friend of yours?"

Linda frowned at her. "Hey, take it easy."

Billie sniffed and continued with her transcript.

There was a little more of that divorce-soon, be-patient-my-darling crap from Hadley, but it didn't seem to be his favorite topic of conversation. He changed the subject to shoptalk, which was what I wanted to hear. Trouble was, he could have shop-talked in Estonian and it would have made just as much sense.

Hadley was concerned about a lengthy "de-con" after a "heapa filter" blew out. There seemed to be some budgetary problem with "jumpers," but somebody named Todd had saved the company a bundle because he didn't panic; he had avoided a "boron dump," whatever that was.

Linda Taree was no help; she said she didn't understand any of the technical terms, either.

Billie licked her lips salaciously and wondered aloud if either of us understood the technical terms from the bedroom part of the tape, terms like "six-shooter" and "honey cave."

"Don't be gross," Linda said, and she shooed Billie out of the office and took her somewhere.

I disconnected all the video gear, coiled cables, and piled the stuff outside the door. When I turned off the lights, Honeybutt's bright office glowed through the big window like life-size TV.

I don't think she could see me in the gloom. She had stopped typing, and she was looking up at my office with a sad and puzzled expression on her face. As clearly as if she had screamed it, her eyes said: I don't understand what is happening now.

I couldn't help her with that one.

I had the same problem.

CHAPTER TWENTY-SEVEN

"You'd swear the building was alive," George said. "It breathes, you know. It rumbles and hisses and moans. See, all the air is sucked in through one vent. Then it flows through the control room and the labs and the hallways and the process cells. The air flows from clean places to dirty places to even dirtier places, and finally it goes through a big duct to the scrubber and out to the atmosphere. Lot of air moving all the time. Noisy air."

George wiped his mouth with a paper napkin and shrugged. "The noise really bothered one guy," he said. "He thought it sounded like the plant was digesting us. He said he knew how Jonah felt."

We were sitting in a booth at Joe Willy's. The table between us was laden with baskets of hamburgers, onion rings, and a galvanized bucket full of ice and Shiner Bock Beer. Joe Willy's was my kind of hamburger joint.

"What you have to understand," George said, "is this: reprocessing nuclear fuel is different from using a reactor to generate power. We're not talking about cheap electricity here; we're talking about manipulating dangerous materials with a K Mart chemistry set."

Geroge—he would not admit to any other name—was a blond guy in his early thirties. He had a short, neatly trimmed beard and a button nose. He had a habit of pausing before he said anything until he had established eye contact.

I snagged another bottle of Shiner and picked up my second Joe Willy burger. Ambrosia. Bliss. Heaven. "As a special favor to a scientific illiterate, George, would you explain what the hell you're talking about?"

George nodded several times while he finished an onion ring. "Well, okay, sure. A nuclear power plant uses fuel, right? That fuel is enriched uranium: pellets of uranium packed into metal tubes about half an inch in diameter. The tubes are long; twelve feet on average. Those tubes are called fuel rods; you've probably heard of them."

"Sure," I said. I'd be okay if he didn't get any more complicated than that.

"The fuel rods are hot; that means radioactive. Now, here's an interesting part," George said. "When fuel rods are used up—what we call "spent"—they're even hotter. I know that doesn't sound logical, but it's true. After spent fuel rods have used up their U-235, they still have lower-grade uranium. And they're contaminated with really bad-news by-products; things like strontium-90 and cesium-137. Plutonium-239, too, and a few others."

"I assume you can't just throw these rod things in the back of a pickup and take them to the dump."

George chuckled ironically. "No way. For one thing, when they come out of the reactor, the rods are not only radioactive, they're physically hot. A couple of hundred degrees minimum, and usually hotter than that. The spent rods have to be stored underwater for six months or so, to cool them down. Power reactors have 'swimming pools' on site, because they replace about a quarter of their fuel rods each year."

I wanted to ask him when the stupid rods would get to Dormac-Chaffee and when he would get to the point, but I held back. Emily Post would have been so proud of me. I settled for prompting. "And after the six months?"

"After that," George said, "there are only two things you can do with the rods. Long-term storage, which is a national disgrace, if you ask me, or reprocessing."

George leaned forward toward me. I smiled around a bite of hamburger to keep him going. He said, "Reprocessing, if it's done properly, could be the answer to the whole nuclear power problem. It would certainly take the load off the storage crisis, because you can recover almost all the fissionable material and reuse it. It's a beautiful cycle. A reprocessing plant recovers the uranium from spent fuel rods. The uranium goes to an enrichment plant, where it's juiced up into U-235. You put that into new fuel rods. It's not perpetual motion, but it's not bad."

"I have this rule, George. Rafferty's Rule Number Forty-one: When someone mentions how good something *could* be, they're really telling me how lousy that something *is*."

George nodded. "Yeah, well, you're right about that. The theory falls down with the reprocessing. The Dormac-Chaffee installation is the second time the U.S. nuclear industry has tried reprocessing spent fuel. The first time was years ago, at the West Valley plant near Buffalo. That one didn't work out too well. For example, West Valley sent one batch of recovered uranium to the enrichment plant in Ohio. Zap! The stuff wasn't clean; they hadn't removed some technetium-99. So the enrichment plant got all gummed up with technetium."

"What the hell is, uh, what-et-ium?"

George gave me a lopsided grin and said, "Come see me when you have a degree in chemistry or nuke physics."

"Okay. Go on, I'm fascinated." Fascinated wasn't quite the word. Worried? Bewildered? Do I hear terrified?

George said, "Not much to go on about. West Valley was shut down eventually. Antinukers raised a stink—about earthquakes, I think—and it would have been too expensive to remodel the plant."

Enough was enough. I stared at him and said, "It's been great fun tiptoeing down the Yellow Brick Road of modern technology with you, George. Now, for God's sake, tell me about the Dormac-Chaffee plant."

George bristled. "It's not safe."

Well, at least he wasn't wishy-washy.

I pushed my empty hamburger basket away and dug out

my pipe and tobacco. I loaded and lit the pipe, went through all that razzamatazz we pipe smokers do, and when I had finished all that, George still had not added anything to "It's not safe."

I said, "*How* is it not safe, George?" He seemed to know the atom business, but it wasn't easy to get him around to the information I wanted.

George held up a finger. "Their de-con and security procedures are worthless, for one thing. The tool—"

"Whoa," I said. "Define 'de-con.' " Hadley had used that word in his taped chat with Cricket.

"Decontamination," George said. "Cleaning contaminated items. Usually, it just means scrubbing and washing with water to remove radioactive particles."

"That's only when something goes wrong, though, isn't it?"

George shook his head. "Not necessarily. Reprocessing is an extremely hot operation. Tools get contaminated during routine maintenance. And tools are like clothes; they're not de-conned because it's cheaper to replace them. That's one area where Dormac-Chaffee screws up. Guys working at the plant, they see wrenches, screwdrivers, and things like that being thrown away because they're a little hot. That gives these geniuses ideas. So they don't throw their tools away anymore, but they still draw new tools from Supply. They take the new tools home, which is no problem because security sucks. And they give the hot tools a quick de-con and keep using them."

"Wonderful," I said. I opened a fresh beer for each of us. Then I got out my list of the confusing terms Hadley had used and smoothed it down on the table. "George," I said, "what's a heapa filter?"

He turned the paper around and peered at it. "You've spelled it wrong. It's HEPA. High Efficiency Particulate Air Filter. It's a big paper filter in that air system I told you about. It strains particulate—radioactive particles—out of the air."

"What would be the effect if a HEPA filter 'blew out?' "

"Depends," he said. "If the filter just ripped a little, the scrubber would probably stop any leakage to the atmosphere.

You'd get away with de-conning the duct and replacing the filter.'' George thought for a moment, and his face became more serious. ''But if the HEPA filter literally blew out; if it broke into hundreds of little scraps of paper, that could be bad. The paper scraps would be hot, and some of them, maybe most, would go up the stack. From there, well, it's just blind luck. On a calm day, the hot stuff might fall inside the plant property where it could be picked up easily. But if there was a good wind blowing . . . why are you asking me this?''

''Didn't Dormac-Chaffee have a blown HEPA filter while you were there?''

I wasn't sure about George. I didn't want to scare him into silence, so I decided to lie to him. Hilda claimed I sometimes made such decisions on insufficient evidence.

''No,'' George said slowly, ''not while I was there.''

''Okay,'' I said, and scurried on to the next item. ''What's a 'boron dump' and why is it expensive?''

''Oh,'' George said, ''well, first I have to tell you how reprocessing works. It's pretty simple, really. The spent fuel is chopped up and dissolved with nitric acid. Then you separate the fission products from the uranium and plutonium, and finally you separate the uranium and plutonium from each other. Anyway, it's a liquid process, and while it's running, you've got this dissolver sloshing with uranium, plutonium, strontium; all that junk the fuel picked up from the reactor.

''Hold that thought,'' George said, ''while I go back to middle school science and teach you how to start a nuclear reaction. Ever hear the term 'critical mass'? That's how. Too much hot stuff—mass—in one place and it goes 'critical'; it begins an uncontrolled nuclear reaction.''

''China syndrome, here we come,'' I said to the melody of ''California, Here I Come.''

George gave me a strange look. ''Yeah, well, anyway, because you might—I said *might*—have a dissolver overloaded one day, there's a tank of boron ready. Boron is a poison to nuclear reactions. So if all that goop starts to go critical, you push a button and the boron drops into the dissolver. Splash—problem solved. Except for one thing; uranium contaminated with boron is useless, so a boron dump into a full dissolver could cost, oh, maybe two or three million dollars.''

"Beats the hell out of glowing in the dark, though," I said.

"Oh, sure," George said seriously. "That's why they put the boron tank there.''

I checked my list and asked George about "jumpers" and why they might be a budget problem. I found out "jumper" was industry jargon for a temporary worker. Jumpers were paid a day's wages for, say, ten minutes' work. The problem was, they were used in areas so contaminated that they picked up a year's permissible radioactivity dosage during their ten-minute workday. George said, "I heard somewhere that Con Ed had to use seventeen hundred welders to repair one pipe failure at Indian Point. How's that for jumpers?''

"I think I've enjoyed almost all of this I can stand," I said. "One last question: is it possible that radioactive material could be missing from the Dormac-Chaffee plant?''

"Oh, hell, yes!" George said. "First off, it's not easy to account for the individual components of the spent fuel. How can I . . . okay, think of it this way. Imagine starting with a bowl of vegetable soup and working backward to determine the exact amount of each ingredient; how much tomato, celery, peas, water, spices, and so on. You know how much soup was in the bowl, but some of the moisture evaporated, and some of the ingredients changed in the cooking, and some stuff is hard to find, let alone measure. After all that, who can say there were twelve and a half grains of salt, not thirteen? You see the problem?''

"Yes, but that's a bookkeeping problem," I said. "What about stealing radioactive material?''

"Simple," said George. "Plutonium would be the thing to take. They make bombs out of it, so there would be big money waiting; Libya, the PLO, whoever. Besides, plutonium would be the easiest item to get out of the plant.''

George was not one of the most fun people I'd ever chatted with.

"Plutonium is deadly," he said, "but only if it gets inside you. If you breathe it in or get it on a cut, you're cactus, but otherwise plutonium is simple to handle. Most of the radiation is alpha. Your skin or a sheet of paper will stop alpha rays, so the container is no real problem.'' George frowned thoughtfully. ''The plutonium at the plant is in liquid form, so I'd use a stainless steel thermos. Pour it carefully, de-con the outside, and you might even sneak it past a counter. Not that it matters. You could tell those security airheads the thermos had leftover coffee in it. There wouldn't be any trouble.''

''It would be that easy?''

George nodded. ''That easy.''

''Have you heard of any radioactive material shortages? Stolen or misplaced, lost or lousy arithmetic, I don't care how; is any of that stuff unaccounted for?''

''I don't know about Dormac-Chaffee,'' George said, ''but you remember that New York reprocessing plant I told you about? West Valley? I read recently that four thousand grams of plutonium was missing from West Valley. Eight pounds, this book said. I don't know if that's true. I hope it's not. I hope there's not eight pounds of plutonium out there somewhere.''

''I'm not sure I really want to know this, George, but how much plutonium does it take to make a bomb?''

George blinked rapidly. ''Not much,'' he said. ''Ten pounds, that's all.'' He looked around at people eating hamburgers, then stared at me. ''Kinda scary when you think about it, huh?''

CHAPTER TWENTY-EIGHT

Outside, in Joe Willy's parking lot, George didn't worry about me seeing which car was his. Maybe he thought using a phoney name meant I couldn't read his license number.

Not that it mattered much; I wasn't going to cause him any problems. But he should have worried about a blue Cavalier that moved out the same time he did. There were two men in the Cavalier. They pretended to ignore me as they followed George out of the lot and into the night.

I left, too, with the Cavalier's license number inked onto the back of my hand and a sudden urge for a phone booth.

I found a booth near a 7-Eleven. I'd barely raised a dial tone when a car killed its lights and eased to the curb fifty yards away. A dark Cavalier. Well, isn't that a coincidence?

I burped the phone to get my money back and walked down the street. They'd parked in a shadow but that didn't make the car invisible. I saw the silhouettes of two men in the front seat, then the license plate.

I was wrong; it wasn't the same Cavalier that had followed George. I wrote down its plate number, though, and went back to the phone booth.

The Dallas Police Department has six patrol stations spotted throughout the city. I had to call three of them before I found a friend from the old days. Jack and I had been rookies together; now he was a lieutenant, a leader of men; a watch commander.

And still a good guy. Jack let the computer chew on the license numbers for thirty seconds, then he told me both Cavaliers were Dormac-Chaffee company cars.

I'd expected that. So why was the back of my neck cold?

I fished around under the front seat of the Mustang, found the jack handle and went visiting.

I was twenty feet from the Cavalier when the driver's window went down.

"Hi, fella. What can we do for you?" a voice said.

I used the jack handle to smash both headlights. The tinkle of glass falling to the pavement sounded a little like wind chimes.

"Well, goddamn!" the voice said.

I went back to the Mustang and drove away. They tried to follow me. Actually, they did a pretty good job of it until I led them down a narrow dark street.

They hit a parked car in the second block.

I woke up early Tuesday morning in a wondering mood.

That phrase—a wondering mood—sounds like it came from a nineteenth-century novel and meant: overcome with a sense of wonder; awed.

But I wasn't awed. I was moody, though, and I wondered how a nice, simple case had gone so screwy so fast?

I banged and clattered around the kitchen, started the coffee pot gargling out caffeine, then leaned against the counter, thinking.

The Dormac-Chaffee kiddie cops hadn't tailed me when we first butted heads six days ago; why start now? Because they had tailed George, I told myself, and they picked me up at Joe Willy's. I wasn't me; I was only someone who contacted George. Whoever George was.

Then I had to gnaw on the question of why Dormac-

Chaffee would tail a disgruntled former employee who hadn't been near the plant for the best part of a year.

The only answer I could come up with was unsettling: they were nervous about something their real or imagined enemies might do. Or had already done?

I poured the first cup of coffee too soon; the final drips popped and sizzled on the hotplate. I took my coffee back to bed; the thinking place.

Pretty goddamned empty thinking place this morning.

After I'd crippled the Cavalier, I hadn't gone to Hilda's as planned. I couldn't take the chance of leading them to her door, and I couldn't be absolutely sure there wasn't a backup team. Even a world-class sneak like me couldn't avoid being tailed if the opposition was willing to devote enough men and equipment to the job.

Hilda had an afternoon flight to St. Louis; another search for antique goodies. I'd miss her, but I wasn't sorry to see her go right now. I'd feel a lot better when she was far away, juggling ormolu chamber pots and pewter ink-wells. At least until I figured out what the hell was going on here.

My concern about keeping Hilda clear of this mess stirred around in my gut with another worry: Dormac-Chaffee and its operations. Between George's description of what *could* happen and Hadley's taped references to what *had* happened, I began to see what Dormac-Chaffee might be afraid of.

And what if there were files to prove it?

I considered that awhile. Was my original argument to Winchester still valid? Probably. The friendly neighborhood atom crunchers could kill the story without killing Cricket Dawes. Couldn't they?

I checked in with my answering service midway through my second cup of coffee. Winchester, Hadley, and Linda Taree. Please call back, all the messages said.

Hell with that, I decided. I'd be seeing Winchester that morning and Hadley could shove it. As for Linda, I was still irritated at Billie, and some of that rubbed off on her. So there.

In that mature and well-reasoned mood, I showered, dressed, and marched off to work with my chest out and my back straight.

Wearing a shoulder holster does wonders for your posture.

CHAPTER TWENTY-NINE

Winchester's Green Army headquarters looked about the same. The place was still crowded, hairy, and earnest. And I had no doubt that Winchester would still be a jerk in an office the size of a phone booth.

There were two differences, though. Linda Taree wasn't working the reception desk, and another Dormac-Chaffee Cavalier—the third so far—was parked across the street. Two men in the front seat tried to pretend they were invisible. *Who, us? Figment of your imagination; we're not here.*

The stupid bastards.

"Rafferty," I told the chubby matron who'd taken Linda Taree's place at the green desk. "To see Winchester."

"And the purpose of your visit?" she prompted.

I hate it when secretaries do that.

I leaned over close and whispered hoarsely, "I have irrefutable evidence that fluoridation of water causes lethal concentrations of navel lint. Tell Winchester."

She looked up at me warily, said, "Wait here," then scurried back to Winchester's office as fast as her sensible shoes could carry her.

After a moment, Winchester poked a pinched, quizzical face out his door. He saw me, rolled his eyes, and wearily waved me toward him. The matron and I crossed paths in the middle of the jumbled office. She went the long way around and banged her hip on a desk because she didn't watch where she was going.

In his office I told Winchester what I'd learned about Dormac-Chaffee, HEPA filters, boron dumps, and other scary stuff. His boyish grin grew broader and broader.

"How much of this can we document?" he said.

I shook my head. "Not a word. I picked up the background dope on how they run things from an anonymous lab technician who used to work there. And the HEPA incident comes from, well, let's call it intercepted transitory data."

He didn't need to know I'd recovered the video. It was an offshoot from something else; that was part of an arrangement with Hadley. Winchester couldn't expect me to—

None of that was true. I just didn't like the thought of Winchester's hairy retinue gawping at Cricket Dawes in the sack. I could imagine newspaper photos and television footage with discreetly blackened areas and snide narration. And Winchester drooling over the publicity.

So, instead of telling him about the video, I changed the subject. "Gimme six hundred bucks."

"What? Six hundred . . ." Winchester had a little trouble changing gears.

"You gave me a three-day advance. That ran out last Wednesday. I worked Thursday, then took a long weekend off. Worked yesterday and today, planning to give it hell tomorrow. Two hundred a day times Thursday, Monday, and today equals six hundred." I smiled at him. "Notice I'm not asking for continued advances. That's because you're an old and cherished customer now."

Winchester did thirty seconds of fish-out-of-water imitations, gave up, and took a checkbook out of his desk drawer. Before he began to write, he looked sideways at me, like he was considering a reprise of the charity-and-chitlins number he'd tried at our first meeting. Then he shook his head twice, bent down, and wrote the check.

I rewarded his penmanship with a complete recap of the

case to date. I leaned hard on the work I was doing to investigate Hadley and Dormac-Chaffee, though I did not tell him the idea was to clear them and show an unknown mugger was responsible for Cricket's death.

I did, however, bite off a big chunk of humble pie and tell Winchester his theory about missing files was looking better and better.

"I don't buy your whole conspiracy package," I said, "but the Dormac-Chaffee security boys have suddenly become very aggressive. Orders to recover missing papers might cause that." I shrugged. "Though I don't know why they didn't start sooner."

Winchester was good; he didn't gloat when I backtracked on the files, and he didn't try to play Inspector Forthright of the Yard.

"Hmm," he said carefully, "what steps do you plan to take now?"

"I'll keep plugging away, with a touch more emphasis on finding those files. Maybe you're—oh, hell, maybe *we're* right. Maybe they do exist."

Winchester nodded. "Things are starting to happen, aren't they? Though I don't understand why Dormac-Chaffee is harassing an ex-employee. And I don't understand why you're withholding his name."

"I'm not withholding it. I don't know it. Truth."

It was, too. I hadn't made a note of George's license number. If I wanted George, I could find him through The Grape. On the other hand, if Winchester wanted him . . . well, life's like that sometimes.

"Hmph," Winchester said. "Oh, say, do you suppose those men out front are . . . ?"

"Dormac-Chaffee security. They got a helluva fleet deal from some hungry Chevy dealer."

"I thought they were cops," Winchester said. He sounded surprised.

I said, "Did they say they were cops; bother your people; anything like that?"

"No," he said. "They took photographs of the volunteers

coming to work, so we took pictures of them." Winchester got a wicked look in his eyes. "This may be good for us, after all. I just assumed they were police, but if they're not, then . . ."

He grinned evilly and reached for the telephone. Funny how he couldn't lift the receiver with my hand over his.

"Hang on there, tiger," I said. "Tell Uncle Rafferty what you have in mind."

"Hey, let go!" He tugged his hand free and waved it around. "Don't you see? We get the news media out here. It's a great story: Green Army harassed by nuclear—"

"That's mental masturbation," I said. "You get a bunch of reporters running around here, and everything will go straight down the tube. They'll tie Cricket Dawes into it faster than you can say 'freedom of the press.' Then Dormac-Chaffee will curl up like an armadillo and tough it out. My lab tech source will disappear. Everyone will dry up.

"We're in my territory now," I told Winchester, "doing things I do well. And I guarantee our best chance to find out the truth is to have everyone out in the open, running around where they're vulnerable."

Our best chance? Did I really say that?

"I want the opposition to myself," I said. "Let's not let a bunch of reporters scare them away."

Winchester tugged at his lower lip. He frowned and sighed and wrestled with it for a few long moments, then said slowly, "Perhaps you're right."

"Trust me. Hey, if those clowns out front bother you, I'll get rid of them."

Winchester sniffed. "Oh, sure you will."

"Watch me."

Winchester caught up with me at the reception desk, where Linda Taree's middle-aged replacement listened with a hesitant look on her round face.

"Call for a tow truck," I said to her. "Tell them to pick up an abandoned car at this address and take it to the Dormac-Chaffee plant. Your files will have the exact address. Tell the tow-truck people the car won't roll, so they should bring a dolly. Oh, and tell them they'll be paid on delivery. By Dormac-Chaffee.''

She looked at me, then at Winchester. He thought, then nodded. She reached for the telephone; I went outside, with Winchester and most of The Green Army office staff following me.

Winchester and his gallant band of brothers lined up on the curb. They watched me take my trusty jack handle out of the Mustang, then cross the street toward the Dormac-Chaffee Cavalier.

The driver was hog-jowled and sixtyish; he had stiff gray-white hair and the look of a retired patrol cop. He also had a handicap; his partner was my old friend Junior, with his broken finger in a splint and his mouth in high gear.

"Watch him, Frank," Junior whined. "He's fast."

"Betcher ass," I said and waggled a forefinger at them. "Out of the car."

Junior said, "No fucking way, hotshot."

"Shut up, kid," Driver said to Junior; then he peered up at me and smiled. "What's the beef, buddy?"

"Citizen's arrest," I said. "The charge against you is feloniously consorting with an asshole." I pointed at the kid. "He's the evidence. Out of the car, both of you."

"Aw, get off it," Driver said.

I used both hands and lots of shoulder to lay the jack handle across the hood of the Cavalier just in front of the windshield. It left a fair trench in the sheet metal. Made a helluva noise, too.

Driver jumped, then said to Junior, "Get out of the car, kid."

"We can take him," Junior said, "easy." He began to reach for something on the floor or under the seat.

I showed them how clean and well oiled I kept the barrel of my .38. Junior froze. Driver slowly put both his hands on top of the steering wheel. He repeated himself to Junior. "Get out of the car," he said. His jaw was somewhat tighter this time.

"And don't—" Driver and I said it together. I let him finish it. "—do anything stupid."

Junior looked bewildered, but he got out peaceably enough. He stood beside the car with his hands up and his splinted finger pointed rigidly skyward. *First of all*, he seemed to be gesturing.

Driver came out slow and easy, making sure I could see his hands every second. "No problem here, buddy," he said to me in a soothing voice. "I didn't survive four tours in South Central Division to get hurt now."

Across the street, in front of The Green Army, someone chanted "pig, pig, pig" in a baritone voice. Then the voice faltered and stopped. "No shit?" the voice said.

Driver and Junior assumed the position and let me pat them down. Driver was clean; so was Junior.

"What happened?" I said to the kid. "Did they take your play-toy away?"

The grimace on Driver's face told me what he thought of Junior carrying firearms.

I put the .38 away then. I felt silly holding a gun on two turkeys like Driver and Junior.

"Okay, boys," I said, "take a hike."

Driver didn't even wait for Junior's response; he grabbed him by the collar, shoved him down the street and took off after him. It wasn't exactly running, but he sure made good time.

Except for Winchester, who stood aloof and calm, The Green Army bunch got a big kick out of that. They jeered and made exaggerated bye-bye waves. A few of them yelled to me. "Aw right!"

I waved to the crowd, got out my pocket knife, and made theatrical gestures with it, like a hammy magician. Then I went around the Cavalier and cut the stems off all four tires. The car jerkily lowered itself to the street, a corner at a time, like an arthritic camel.

Up the block, Junior looked back over his shoulder, then yelled at Driver. Junior didn't stop walking, though. Driver didn't even turn around to look.

The Green Army crowd cheered at me. All except Winchester; he scowled and turned for the door.

I took a bow. The crowd cheered again. It was kind of fun.

CHAPTER THIRTY

"Going to miss me?" Hilda asked.

"Imagine losing an arm," I said. "That'll give you a rough idea."

We were sitting in an open cocktail bar in the American terminal at Dallas–Fort Worth, killing time until Hilda's flight. The bar was out in the open; only a different carpet color and a low railing distinguished it from the rest of the terminal.

There were no signs of undue interest from the crowd. I kept watching anyway. A sharp guy like me can keep watch and drink at the same time. I had a large cold mug of Amstel Light, which went down well. Hilda had a margarita, which did not.

"Too much lime," she said. "Rafferty, will you stop scowling at that man? What's the matter with you?"

"Sorry." I told Hilda I wasn't entirely desolate about her buying trip; in fact, having her out of town while I finished the Dawes case sounded pretty good.

"That's why I wanted us to bring both cars out here," I said, "so I could, ahem, watch your rear. And, speaking of your rear, may I just say—"

"It doesn't seem very amusing to me," she said.

"Well, look, Hil, I'm probably overreacting. Humor me,

162

will you? If this brouhaha still isn't settled when you get back, I want Mimi to move in with you.''

Hilda frowned. ''I like Mimi,'' she said, ''even if she does talk about guns and horses all the time. But why her? Why don't you . . . oh, I see.''

''Right. I can protect you at home, but I can't end the need for protection. So Mimi could look after you, while Cowboy and I . . . well, negotiated the peace, you might say.''

Hilda chugged down the margarita she didn't like and said, ''Let's go. They'll be calling my flight in a minute.'' As we left the bar, she sighed heavily.

On the way to her gate I said, ''Don't worry, babe. There's no evidence they even know about you. And they're sure as hell not going to try a snatch in this crowd.''

She leaned against me. ''You dummy. I'm worried about you, not me.''

I turned her out of the crowd and backed her into a corner. I held her shoulders and kissed her forehead. ''How you do carry on,'' I said. ''You should know how carefully I look after this scarred, but still magnificent, body.''

She rolled her eyes skeptically. ''The hell you do.''

''But I do. For example, at this very minute I am wearing the newest personal protection device known to mankind. Very chic; extremely high tech.''

There was a tiny lift to the corners of her mouth, but her eyes remained heavy and shiny.

''Absolutely the latest thing in body armor,'' I said. ''Bulletproof underwear.''

''Rafferty,'' she said, with the Hilda grin starting to show through, ''you're crazy.''

''It's true,'' I said. ''Seventeen layers of Kevlar. Total protection for the family jewels. Go ahead, cop a feel, you'll see.''

''You cannot be serious.'' She looked around me at the crowd swirling past. ''If anybody sees this . . . Rafferty! You—!''

''Nice,'' I said, ''do it again. This time, squeeze rhythmically and murmur sexy things in my ear.''

She didn't; she hit me in the stomach instead, but she was

smiling and relaxed when she went down the plastic tunnel to the plane. That's what counted.

Me? I went back to Dallas, to—as Cowboy would say—kick me some ass. I even had an appointment to do it. How's that for uptown?

CHAPTER THIRTY-ONE

Walter Hadley opened the front door of his four hundred twenty-five thousand dollar zero-building-line Executive Haven. "Come in," he said, "come on in. Good to see you."

He was hail-fellow-well-met and cheery, but his eyes had a bright, almost frantic, intensity. He showed me to his wife. He told her I was a labor-relations guy from the head office and we had to meet at home so the unions didn't catch on, and you just run along, dear, don't mind us.

Ann Hadley was a handsome woman, with a squared-off jawline and worried eyes. She didn't believe a single word Hadley said. I liked her immediately.

Hadley marched me through five thousand square feet of Home Show glitz. It was plush and desirable, the sort of house most folks dream of. Except for the tension that crackled in every corner. Imagine the atmosphere twenty minutes before a prison riot; you'll be pretty close.

Hadley led me to a room he called his study and closed the door behind us. He paused with his back to me for a second, then turned with a big smile. "Thanks for coming over," he said. "You, uh, ought to do something about your answering service, though. I've been leaving messages for days."

"I got all the messages," I said.

"Oh." His smile went away. "Well. Um, I want to talk to you about, oh, one thing and another."

We sat down in mock leather chairs on each side of a spindly table. Hadley smiled at me, and I looked at him. Finally I got tired of that, so I said, "What's your problem? Did Nagle show up with another copy of your video *Kama Sutra*?"

Hadley winced and shot a glance at the closed study door. "Keep it down. No, I haven't heard from Nagle, thank God. But, well, I have an offer for you. A very generous offer, I think."

"It better be generous if you expect me to sell you those files," I said firmly. Sometimes you have to swing for the long ball if you want to stay in the game.

Hadley's face told me everything I wanted to know, but he went on and talked about it, anyway. "Whew!" he said, "that's a relief. I thought perhaps . . ."

It occurred to me too late that by pretending to have the files, I'd blown any chance of finding out what the files contained. Ah, well. You win some; you lose some.

I said, "Just hold your 'generous offer' for a moment. I won't deal until I know exactly how they went missing."

Hadley raised his hands in friendly surrender. "All right. We're together on this, I can see that," he said and lowered his voice. "You were right. What you guessed the day you stopped me with that fake flat tire charade, I mean. About, oh, a week before Cricket died, I came out of my office and found her with several confidential files on her desk. She was going through them, making a list of the files she wanted to steal."

"You mean she took originals? Why not photocopy them when you weren't looking?"

Hadley shrugged. "I—I don't know," he said. "Copy room security, maybe. They keep track of . . . or, well, perhaps she wanted to spite me; make me look foolish." He shrugged again and slumped lower in his chair. His executive camaraderie had given out.

"Go on."

Hadley put the ends of his thumbnails together and flicked

them. The process made a soft clicking sound. While he talked, he watched his thumbs make the sound.

"I confronted her, of course," he said quietly. "We had an argument. A bitter, personal argument. She accused me of lying to her about—well, the details don't matter. The main thrust of her argument was defiance; she said she would take any and all the company documents she wanted, when and where she wanted to take them. And if I tried to stop her, she would let—she would embarrass me with that video we made."

Hadley raised his head and looked at me. "What could I do? I didn't know why she wanted the company files, but honestly, I didn't even think about that part of it. I was shocked—and worried—about her threat; about the possibility of Ann seeing that tape. So I didn't call Security. Instead, I told myself I could talk Cricket out of it before she actually took anything.

"Then," Hadley said, "a week or so later, I heard that Cricket was dead. I went to the office early the next morning and checked the files. She'd taken the P-239 Separation Logs, a final report on an external decon from a HEPA—well, I don't have to tell you what she took. You know." He laughed a hollow false laugh. "And I'm glad to know where they are, believe me."

Me? Say anything at that point? No way.

"I didn't know what to do that morning," Hadley said. "Confidential files—damaging files in the wrong hands—were gone. And that damned video was in with Cricket's things, waiting to be found. Eventually, I hired Nagle." He grimaced. "You know what a lousy idea that was. And while Nagle still had the video, I kept quiet about the missing files. That was foolish, I know that now, but I was afraid a thorough search for the files would uncover the video. Then, after you got it away from Nagle, I pretended to discover the files were missing. The company believes me. I think."

"Wonderful. You've belatedly reported they were stolen without your knowledge by a dead girl who screwed you silly on a video you have finally covered up," I said.

"What do you do for light entertainment, Hadley, torture kittens?"

Hadley sighed. "Go ahead. I deserve it; I was wrong. But listen, I can offer you—"

"Not yet," I said. "Let's tie up a few loose ends here. Do I have this right? After you finally reported the file theft, the company rent-a-cops kicked into high gear. And that's why I keep stumbling over dark Cavaliers with multiple morons in them."

"Yes," he said. "Corporate Security—they're a different division from mine; I'm Materiel Security—they had some suspicions about Cricket's death. But that's just the way they are; they act like the CIA or something. Anyway, when I eventually reported the files missing, Corporate Security did the usual internal checks; then they started external operations."

Hadley said it like "external operation" was a natural process; sunshine, rainfall, external operation, that sort of thing.

"Define 'external operations,' " I said.

"Well, for one thing, they're watching former employees who have turned against us. You'd be amazed how ungrateful people can be. You fire some loser, and the first thing you know, he's in bed with some lunatic ecology group. Oh, Corporate Security is watching the groups, too, to identify any members who might be ex-employees. And to look for conservationists we could convert, that sort of thing."

Obviously he hadn't heard about the fun and games at The Green Army's office that morning.

" 'Convert,' " I said. "That means bribe, I suppose."

Hadley shrugged and screwed his face into a phoney frown. "Well . . ."

"Never mind," I said, "what made you decide I have the files?"

"I hadn't," Hadley said. "That's the funny part. I was going to offer you the job of finding them. And then when you said—"

"I lied," I said. "I just wanted to confirm they were actually missing."

Hadley didn't like that.

"You've cleared up a lot for me," I said. "It's beginning to look like the killer has—or had—the files." I had a sudden flash of a disgruntled mugger pawing through boring technical papers, then dumping them down a sewer.

Hadley, bitter now: "Well, I don't have them. And I didn't kill her, either. Why don't you and the cops leave me the hell alone?"

"Oh ho," I said, "cops been asking nasty questions, have they?"

He didn't like that, either.

"Who interviewed you?" I said. "Sergeant Ricco? Skinny little guy, dresses like a South Dallas pimp?"

"I don't know," Hadley mumbled, "that sounds like him."

"What are you bitching about? You're not in the slammer."

Hadley shook his head. "I don't see why I should have to put up with that kind of treatment. I haven't done anything wrong."

"Yeah, well, I'll tell you, Wally, there's something about this whole goddamn mess that really gets up my nose. Nobody seems to have done anything terribly wrong, but Cricket Dawes is still dead."

I told him how Cricket had bumped her head and drowned, unconscious, because of a lousy nosebleed.

"Oh, my God," he said, and swallowed heavily. I thought for a minute he was going to vomit. He held it in, though, while he got up and lurched to a liquor cabinet built into his expensive bookshelves. Walter stood with his back to me while he poured and knocked down a triple shot of Chivas, no ice, no finesse. Then he carefully reloaded the glass, added ice, and carried it back to his chair. He didn't offer me one.

"I had no idea," Walter said. "I—I assumed a gun. Or a knife, something like that." He shuddered and gulped half of his second drink.

We sat there for a long time without saying anything. Walter drank and I thought.

It was about time Hadley had reacted to Cricket's death. Up to now he had been pretty cool. And, after all, she had been his lover. Hadley should care, if anyone did.

And then there was Winchester; another charmer. He had been using Cricket to promote his political views. Yet, until now, I seemed to be more concerned about her death than Hadley and Winchester combined.

I decided, weighing all the available evidence, that I might be considered maudlin, but Hadley was a scumbag. Winchester, too.

"Anyway," I said to Hadley, "word is, you're in the clear. Whoever bopped her on the nose, it wasn't you."

Hadley's look mixed quizzical with queasy.

"I talked to Ricco before I came out here," I said. I had called Ricco to verify that the files hadn't been found in Cricket's car. They hadn't, Ricco told me; the car was clean. Then he told me about the alibi Hadley didn't realize he had.

It seemed the Dormac-Chaffee gate guards logged company heavies like Hadley in and out of the plant. It was all part of some fancy procedure for locating key personnel in case of emergency. Ricco had seen the log. "With my own eyes," he had said. "And stay the hell outta my way," he had also said. He says that a lot.

"Anyway," I told Hadley now, "the log for that Friday shows you didn't leave the plant until after Cricket's body was found."

Hadley slowly wagged his head, as if to clear it.

"Which is good news for you," I said, "because otherwise—what with the video, the stolen files, and all that—you'd be a prime suspect. And you wouldn't be bitching about Ricco, you'd be begging to be interrogated by him, instead of me. Because Ricco's a real cop. He has to be nice.

"I don't have to be nice," I said, "especially to a slug like you. Me, I would tap-dance on your testicles until you talked.'' I stepped out a quick shave-and-a-haircut-two-bits rhythm on the carpet in front of my chair.

Hadley did throw up that time.

Afterward he looked a little better, but the bone-colored carpet was pretty gruesome.

CHAPTER THIRTY-TWO

"Don't know why we didn't get them goddamn papers in the first place," Cowboy grumbled. "Those old boys are gonna be all stirred up and feisty now."

Cowboy slouched in the passenger seat of the Mustang and thumbed fat cartridges into his Ruger Super Blackhawk. Mimi had phoned with the "go" signal, and we were headed north on Central Expressway. It was almost midnight. We were—to use a phrase I heard often as a boy—up to no good.

"It's just too bad if they are feisty," I said. "When we took the video away from Nagle last week, I didn't believe there *were* any files. Now I know there are. Mea culpa."

Cowboy put the Ruger on the seat beside him and began filling speed-loaders. "Wish you'd lay off that Latin shit," he said. "Gonna tell me that one means 'kick ass,' too? Like excelsior?"

"Sure. Ancient Romans had an unhealthy fixation with the phrase."

"Oh, yeah," Cowboy said. "Cicero, Juvenal, Pliny, all them old boys. Bunch of maladjusted, sadistic sociopaths. I knowed that for years."

Every so often, Cowboy nails me with a zinger like that.

The Mockingbird Lane exit swam into the headlights. I drove up the exit ramp and turned right.

172

"Anyhow," Cowboy said, smiling to himself, "what makes you so sure this Nagle dude has the files?"

"I'm not at all sure he has them," I said. "I'm just working my way through the possibilities."

"You want a prime possibility, Rafferty, you find the mugger who whacked your pal Cricket. He probably saw the files, thought they was valuab'e, and took 'em when he grabbed her purse."

We made the light at Mockingbird and Greenville. I turned left.

"Hell," I said, "whoever whacked Cricket is high on my list, too, but we don't know she had the files in her car that Friday. Hadley says she began stealing them—or began preparing to steal them, anyway—a week earlier. She might have taken them any day. Or maybe she took a few items on each of several different days. Point is, they may have been hidden in a part of the apartment I hadn't searched before I was, uh, interrupted."

"All right," Cowboy said. "S'pose that's so. S'pose the files were in her apartment, not her car. When that Nagle dude took the video away from you, why didn't he take the files, too?"

Cowboy pointed to a street going left. I turned into it. A block and a half later we wheeled into an alley. I killed the headlights and let the Mustang idle along at a walking pace. The parking lights showed us the bottom half of a solid wood fence that changed color and condition at each property line.

"Well," I said, "maybe Nagle already had the files."

Cowboy shook his head. "That don't make no sense. Nagle wouldn't have gone to that apartment for the files one time, then gone back for the video. There ain't no way he would have known anything about that company or files or any of that stuff until Hadley hired him to git the video. And from what you said, the video wasn't hid good enough for Nagle to miss it. That means the night you saw him, that was his first time at that apartment. He didn't look for the files then because he didn't know about them. Betcha."

I stopped near a narrow opening in the fence. We got out of the Mustang, then reached back in for the shotguns on the rear seat. Cowboy slipped his big Ruger into a holster that reached almost to his right knee. He put three full speed-loaders into fat pouches on the gunbelt.

I jammed my .45 into the back of my belt. I'm on the low tech end of my trade.

We went through the fence opening, across the back parking lot of Fulvio's, and stopped in a deep shadow that masked the back door.

"I see what you mean about Nagle," I said. "The files might still be in Cricket's apartment."

Cowboy said, "Yep. Or he might have gone back and gotten them since. Though I don't see how he would know about them now, if he didn't know about them at first."

I tried Fulvio's back door. Unlocked; Mimi was on the ball tonight. Cowboy and I stepped into one end of a long, poorly lit corridor and let the door close behind us. The far end of the corridor turned right and—to judge from the light and noise—opened onto Fulvio's sprawling barrooms.

Mimi appeared from around the corner. She held up her right hand in a "stop" gesture, checked behind her, then hurried down the corridor toward us.

"I'll tell you how Nagle might have tumbled to the files," I said. "Hadley is a turkey. When he hired Nagle to get the video, he'd have been huffy and secretive. But once Nagle had the video and opened blackmail proceedings . . . Well, hell, I can see Hadley going all panicky and talkative."

Mimi stopped halfway down the corridor, in front of a closed door. She raised her finger to her lips, then opened her oversize bag and took out a silenced Uzi. She extended the folding stock, braced herself opposite the door, and nodded. Cowboy and I tiptoed forward.

"Well, what it boils down to then is this," Cowboy whispered. "We don't even know how much we know. And that's why we gotta get Nagle's heart thumpin' so hard he'll tell the truth 'bout whether or not he's got them files. Right?"

The door had OFFICE written on it with those fake gold leaf decals you can buy at stationery stores. I put my ear against the wood. There was music playing in the office. I thought I heard the low drone of conversation, too, but it was difficult to be certain.

I whispered to Cowboy, "You're right about the plan, but it sounds kind of flabby when you say it out loud like that."

"Ah, hell, boss man," Cowboy hissed back, "it ain't such a bad plan. And you never know, there might be enough opposition in here to make it interesting." He raised one booted foot and kicked the door beside the knob. Hard. Twice.

The door flew open and banged against the wall. I went in first, with Cowboy close behind me. And I knew Mimi would be behind him, covering the central killing zone from the doorway.

And then we were inside, "amongst 'em," as Cowboy would say, and it would have all gone down very smoothly and calmly if one of Nagle's goons hadn't decided he was immortal.

CHAPTER THIRTY-THREE

The office was fair sized and plush, especially compared to the low-life decor in the public part of that gin joint.

There was a large smooth-faced man—Fulvio?—behind an ornate dark-timber and black-wrought-iron desk. He banged the desk top angrily.

Nagle was there, too, lounging comfortably in a black leather chair pulled up to the side of that aircraft carrier-sized desk.

And one of Nagle's goons was there; not the mental midget who'd lost part of his hand to Cowboy's shotgun, but another no-neck mouth-breather with delusions of adequacy.

No-neck had a stainless Colt Python halfway out of a shoulder holster when I said, "Don't! You can't win this one!"

I wasn't kidding. I'd gone low and left, Cowboy high and right; Mimi blocked the doorway: Mighty Mouse with a submachine gun. Let's face it, by suburban Dallas standards, it was a damned good imitation of the Normandy landing.

No-neck paused with the Python free of the holster but pointed at his own armpit. He still had a choice.

"Easy," I said. "We can do this without anybody getting hurt."

Nagle's voice had a little catch in it as he said, "Randy. Don't push your—"

Nagle probably meant to finish that sentence with the word "luck," but Randy No-Neck couldn't wait to use up the last of his. He started the Python moving again, and he seemed to be going all the way with it.

Mimi shot Randy in the chest with a short burst from the Uzi. Three rounds; Mimi always did handle automatic weapons well. Good fire discipline.

Good silencer, too. The only noises that Uzi made were a soft rapid *chug-chug-chug* sound and the rattle of the bolt. Randy's arms went limp, like a puppet with cut strings. He slumped against the wall and slid down to the floor. The front of him didn't look too bad, but his back left quite a mess on the wallpaper.

Cowboy had Fulvio and Nagle covered. I looked at Mimi, and she backed out into the corridor. Ten seconds later she came back and nodded the all clear.

"Now," I said to Nagle, "as I was about to mention before we were so rudely interrupted, we've come to make a deal for the Dormac-Chaffee files."

Elmo Nagle did not look well. His face was pale and he breathed rapidly. "What . . . um, file is that?" he said. He couldn't stop glancing at Randy's body, slumped in the corner with its chin on its chest.

"Files plural," I said. "The ones you found in Cricket's apartment."

"Oh, uh," Nagle said, "those files." He looked at Fulvio. Fulvio didn't look back; he just sat behind his big desk, with his hands on his leather-backed blotter. His dark eyes clicked from Cowboy to Mimi to me and back again.

Nagle tentatively raised his right hand and wiped his face. "Well, hell's bells, old hoss," he said, "you didn't need to go to all this trouble just to talk." The jaunty words didn't fit with the tremble in his voice. "Why, sure, we can make a deal."

"I'll give you twenty thousand," I said. "We do the exchange tomorrow night. You choose the place, but we'll refuse unless you come up with a good spot. Open, public, neutral territory. Deal?''

Nagle squirmed. ''Well, hoss, I don't know if I can get them out that soon. Got 'em salted away pretty good, you know. Valuable stuff.'' He wiped his face again.

''Don't jerk me around, Nagle. If you can't get the files in twenty-four hours, you don't have them.''

''Well, of course, I—'' Nagle rubbed his chest now, with the heel of his hand. He seemed to be pressing very hard. Finally he shook his head. ''No,'' he said. ''Forget it. I don't know what you're talking about, and I don't want to know.''

''Let's go,'' I said.

Mimi darted out into the corridor. Cowboy went behind Fulvio's desk and jerked two phone lines out of the wall. There was a wireless intercom on the desk, too. He put that on the floor and stomped it into small plastic bits.

Mimi called softly, ''Clear.''

Cowboy and I backed out of the office. I pulled the shattered door closed and waited two steps down the corridor to see if any heads would appear. None had by the time Cowboy whistled from the back door, so I joined him and Mimi there.

We all went across the parking lot, out through the fence, got into the Mustang and drove away.

''Well,'' Cowboy said, ''now you know he ain't got 'em. What next, boss man?''

''The apartment, I guess. I'll toss it tomorrow.'' I glanced at the dashboard clock. ''Later today. After I sleep. You know what I mean.''

''Rafferty,'' Mimi said, ''you want those files out in public, don't you? I know they might lead you to whoever killed that girl, and I know you're a big old mean sucker, but there's something about letting people know what's happening at that atomic place all mixed up in here, too, isn't there?''

''Come on, Mimi, I'm no do-gooder. This is just another investigation, that's all.''

''Don't get him started, Mimi,'' Cowboy said. ''He'll make up a buncha fancy Latin stuff.''

"Now, would I do that?" I said.

"Yep," Cowboy said, "you get all dewy-eyed and foolish whenever you get into this *pro bono publico* shit."

Mimi giggled.

CHAPTER THIRTY-FOUR

I slobbed around the house for a while the next morning, drinking coffee and wondering what Hilda was doing in St. Louis. She was doubtless hard at work already, I decided. She wouldn't have stayed up late terrorizing bent ex-cops. Well, probably not, anyway.

On my third cup of coffee, I started the day's labors. Item one on the agenda was getting into Cricket's apartment. I thought about Stanley Mellish, doughy manager of the Casa Cahuenga; fleshy guardian of the apartment the cops wanted sealed up.

Mellish might be bribable, but it was iffy. I decided to con him, instead. He'd appreciate that. Surely, Stanley would rather have people think he was gullible than think he was crooked.

And for my end of it, I'd figure out a way to square it later with Ed Durkee. I usually did.

I phoned Mellish and told him I was Sergeant Jim Hackstanding, Dallas Police Department. I also told Mellish he should let my good friend and confidant Rafferty into the Dawes apartment. "No one else," I said, "but, well, Rafferty's giving us a hand with the case. He's one of the best, you know."

Okay, okay, so I got carried away.

"Well-l-l," Stanley Mellish said. I could imagine his big white hands dancing and hopping around.

"Would you like to call me back?" I said. "For confirmation? Can't be too careful, you know."

Mellish liked that idea. I gave him my phone number, hung up, and counted slowly to myself.

On eight, the phone rang. I let Mellish talk to Hackstanding again, but not until after I held my nose and did thirty seconds of "Officer Rockhampton" answering phones and bitching about summer colds.

I've always believed it's the little extra touches that add versimilitude to a telephone con.

Thirty minutes later I was backing out of the driveway when Linda Taree's Volkswagen pulled up, clattering and beeping.

She got out and trotted to the side of the Mustang. I rolled the window down and scowled out at her.

"Hi," she said cheerily, "how you doing? What's the matter?"

"I thought I was mad at you for dragging that Billie character around to my office, but I just realized that's not fair." I found a smile somewhere and showed it to her. "So I'm fine. How're you? And I'm sorry I can't chat, but I'm off to work now."

Linda sat on her heels beside the car. She balanced herself with one hand on the door handle. "Well, hey, don't rush off. Are you still working on the Dawes thing?" She smiled broadly. "Tell me all about it. I'm intrigued."

I thought for a moment, mostly examining my motives. When I passed muster, I said, "I'm off to shake down Cricket's apartment. You can come along if you want."

She jumped up, excited, then slumped. "Aw, hell," she said, "I better not. I'm, uh, looking for a job, and I have this interview in about an hour. I better do the right thing. But, hey, thanks very much for asking me."

"Okay, then," I said. "Gotta go. The forces of evil are a-march."

As I backed into the street, Linda Taree waved, then got

into her VW. I saw her behind me a block later, then she disappeared in the traffic.

4:08 P.M. I sat on the couch in Cricket's apartment and wondered what I had done to deserve this. I was sweaty, I was tired, and I was confused. I had been so sure I would find the Dormac-Chaffee files. I'd have bet big money on that. Which is why bookies drive Cadillacs and I drive an old Mustang, I guess.

I had tried everywhere I could think of. Under mattresses and dresser drawers and carpets. Inside frozen food boxes and folded bathtowels and furniture cushions. On top of kitchen cabinets and ceiling vents and the refrigerator. I even went through a now-old newpaper she hadn't thrown out, in case she was a *Purloined Letter* fan.

Finally, after four and a half hours of searching, I had come to the sad-but-true part; there weren't any files here.

You have no idea how much it hurt to admit that.

I shuffled down to the office and gave Stanley Mellish the key.

"Come back any time," Mellish said. His hands hopped agreement. "Any time. Sergeant Hackstanding said it was all right."

"Yeah, salt of the earth, old Jim." I left.

Behind the Casa Cahuenga, I stood in Cricket's parking slot and looked up and down the alley.

She drove down the alley and turned in here, I thought. She got out of the car and—

And what? Someone bopped her on the nose and she fell down. Her purse disappeared, doubtless with the bopper. And the files? Because if the files weren't in her apartment—and never had been—then bopper must have taken them.

If bopper was a mugger, I was back to my first theory. It had a tortuous uphill feel to it.

So imagine a mugger. Bop, grab-grab, and away. A purse means money; he'd keep that. But the files? How far would he run before he opened the envelope or bag or folder, whatever it was, and saw it was only papers? A block? A half block?

I went down the alley to the right. I peered behind scraggly bushes and pawed through weed patches and looked into backyards. All I needed was one piece of paper.

I opened garbage cans. They had been emptied two or three times since Cricket died, but maybe something had stuck to the bottom or side or . . . one piece of paper, that was all, just to show me I was right.

That half of the alley was a total loss. I went back past the Casa Cahuenga and tried the other end.

This end of the alley had been my escape route the night I burgled Cricket's place. Maybe the mugger had used it, too.

Then I remembered a third person who used this alley; a person who might have seen Cricket die; a person who at least might have found her purse. Or even the files, if I was very lucky.

I found that person twenty minutes later, but it was hard to imagine him telling me anything about how Cricket died. At first glance, he looked pretty dead himself.

CHAPTER THIRTY-FIVE

Only his legs from the calf down protruded from under a dusty hedge beside the alley. He was facedown and still as death. Or a recently flush wino. I knelt, poked his leg, and said, "Hey, old-timer."

Nothing. I did it again. Still nothing.

Hell with this, I thought. If he's dead, it won't hurt him, and if he's not, it'll wake him up. I grabbed his bare ankles and dragged him out of the hedge. From the smell that came with him, I thought he was a corpse.

I was wrong. The gravel rash awakened him, and he thrashed his way into a sitting position.

"Goddam commie sumbitch," he muttered. "Git over here; gonna beat shit otta ya." He sat there, blinking and swearing, with his legs out straight in front of him, and he flailed his toothpick arms at empty air.

I couldn't tell whether or not he was the same wino I had quieted down during my getaway last week. Even to a superbly trained supersleuth like me, winos tend to look alike.

"Calm down, old-timer," I said. I fished a five dollar bill out of my wallet and dangled it just out of his reach. "I have your next jug or two here, as soon as you answer some questions."

He squinted ferociously. Behind the stubble and grimy wrinkles, a massive effort took place. His rheumy gray eyes locked onto the five. He shuddered, smacked his lips, grunted, and said in a surprisingly low, even voice, "Begin, my good man."

"Okay. About two weeks ago, there was some excitement at the apartment building down there. There were police cars, an ambulance, probably people walking up and down the alley here. Do you remember that day?"

It took a while, but it got through. "Yes," he said, "I think I do."

"Good. Pay attention now. I want to know what happened *before* the excitement. Did you see a woman drive a white Corolla into the apartment parking lot?"

He thought, then shook his head slowly.

"Little Japanese car," I said. "A young blond woman."

He kept shaking his head. He didn't stop until I told him to do so. "It's all right if you didn't see her," I said, "don't worry about it. Just don't say yes to anything unless you're sure."

He tossed a worried look at the five.

"I'll pay you whether you say yes or no," I said. "Just be sure you tell me the truth. Next question: did you see anyone here in the alley before the police cars came? Someone walking, maybe carrying a purse or a package. Maybe both."

He looked like he was saddened because he had to shake his head no again.

"Okay," I said, even though it wasn't. "You're doing fine. Now let's talk about all the days since the excitement. Got that? From when the excitement happened to right now, okay?"

He nodded.

"Have you found a purse or a package of papers since then?"

Headshake. Sad look, but no.

"Do you know if anyone else has found a purse or papers?"

Headshake no.

A desperation move. "Do you spend most of your time here? In this alley?"

"Yes." Spoken this time, in that strange nonwino voice.

By then I was willing to make a guess based on what he hadn't seen, so I said, "If you're here most of the time, then you know everything that happens, right?"

Tragic, slow headshake. "No," he said. He sat up a trifle straighter. "You see, I drink."

I gave him the five and started to walk away. Then I turned back, gave him another five and helped him over to the side of the alley. Someone might run over the poor old bastard if he stayed where he was.

When I started to leave him for the second time, he grabbed my sleeve with one filthy claw. "The astronomer," he said. "Try him. The astronomer might have seen those things you want to know."

"Who is the astronomer?"

He scrabbled at a fence and pulled himself upright, creakily started down the alley and said in his loudest voice so far, "Follow me. Enlightenment awaits."

A few moments later the old wino pointed a wobbly arm at a weathered frame house that backed onto the alley opposite the Casa Cahuenga. A second-story window was open.

"There," he said, with a ragged flourish. "The astronomer. On duty as always."

I could just make out a round black cylinder a foot or so inside the open window. It was a telescope, mounted to overlook the apartment building and its parking lot. Hot damn!

I shook the old man's hand, despite the grime and the smell, and gave him another ten bucks.

He took it with formal grace. "You do realize," he intoned, "that 'astronomer' is my little joke. I believe the operator of that device is a voyeur. A peeping, er, ah . . ."

"Tom," I said.

He blinked, then frowned thoughtfully for several seconds. Finally he inclined his head and said, "Good day to you, Tom. Ralph Wilkston, at your service."

CHAPTER THIRTY-SIX

There was a six-foot timber fence, gone gray with age, where the voyeur's house backed onto the alley. There was a locked gate. I leaned against the gate, something popped sharply, and then it wasn't locked anymore.

The enclosed backyard was a jungle of overgrown bushes and high grass. I couldn't help wondering about snakes as I waded through the scrub.

When I went around the front corner of the sprawling old house, the scrub thinned out, and a metallic clacking sound began. Then someone called, "Where do you think you're going, young man?"

She was seventy, perhaps, and wiry. She looked old enough to make erratic snap decisions and determined enough to act upon those decisions. She had been clipping thorny limbs off a hugely overgrown rosebush.

Now, she clacked the long-bladed clippers open and shut like a weapon. "State your business," she snapped.

I took out my wallet and flipped it open and shut. All I showed her—for a quarter of a second—was my last parking ticket and a picture of Hilda, but people often buy that gimmick. Too much television, I think.

She scowled in disgust and let the clippers dangle from one thin leathery arm. "Can't say I'm surprised," she said. "You're here for Norwood, aren't you?"

I said, "Is Norwood the, ah . . . ?" I pointed at the second floor of the house and mimed looking through a telescope.

She nodded. "Kids! They never listen. I told him this'd happen." She inhaled fiercely through her nose and turned back to the rosebush. "Go on up," she said. "Just don't hurt him. He can't help it. Norwood's not . . . quite right."

She wriggled the clipper blades over a rosebush branch and whacked the handles closed. She didn't say anything, but I had the distinct feeling she wished that branch was Norwood's neck. Or his scrotum.

I went up the front steps to a wide porch that needed a fresh coat of paint on the floor timbers. There was a wooden screen door—how long has it been since you've seen one of those?—and a dark, heavy front door with stained glass panels beside it and a fanlight above.

Inside, a wide staircase climbed up and away from the entrance hall. I started up. The banister was dark and smooth from years of use, and the steps creaked a little. I stepped on the outside edges of the treads to cut down the noise and wondered about that "Norwood's not quite right" remark.

On the second floor I worked out where that window had to be and moved toward the appropriate room. I didn't take out the .38, but I did loosen it in its holster.

Then I stepped into the doorway.

It might have been a bedroom once, or a study or a nursery; I couldn't tell. The wallpaper was long past evoking a mood, and there was almost no furniture. The only things I saw were a cheap card table, a chair, and the telescope on its tripod.

And Norwood, of course.

When I knocked on the open door, he lifted his face from the telescope and turned slowly. He was forty, give or take, broad shouldered and baby-fat plump, with a shock of brown hair and a vacant moon face.

Norwood raised his right hand, palm forward, to shoulder level and waved it back and forth twice. "Hi," he said. He smiled at me. It was a pleasant smile, but his eyes didn't seem to realize exactly what the rest of his face was doing.

"Hi, Norwood," I said. I pointed at his telescope. "Mind if I take a look?"

"Huh? Oh! Oh, sure, go ahead," he said. He hopped clumsily out of the way, and bumped the rickety card table. A short stack of magazines fell off the table and flopped onto the floor.

The telescope was pointed across the alley toward the Casa Cahuenga. I squinted through the eyepiece and quickly straightened up again. I didn't like exposing the back of my neck to Norwood, for one thing, and for another, I didn't need a long look. I recognized the couple from the apartment pool. I also recognized what they were doing on their bedroom floor.

"Those Thirty-sevens," Norwood said with a merry giggle. "Aren't they something?"

"Really something," I said. "Norwood, I want to ask you a few—"

He was gone by then, hunched over the telescope again. Every few seconds his shoulders jumped and he made a soft sound halfway between a cough and a chuckle.

Why me? I thought. Why don't I ever get to question nuns, librarians, accountants; people like that?

I picked up the magazines Norwood had knocked onto the floor and dropped them on the table. They were mostly the soft porn "men's" magazines you see everywhere, but mixed in with them was a dog-eared notebook; the kind kids use for schoolwork. On the front, someone had carefully scrawled "Norwood A. Kempler," and below that, "His Book."

It was a log of Norwood's, er, sightings. The first entry was dated eleven months earlier. I offered myself very good odds there was a tall stack of books that preceded this one.

Norwood's penmanship would have worried a fourth-grade teacher, and he favored smeary pencils, but I could read most of it. The constant references to numbers confused me at first, then I realized he was using the Casa Cahuenga apartment numbers because he didn't know their names.

Once I thought about that, and saw that Norwood seemed conscientious about the days and dates, I went straight to Friday the ninth.

There it was, all laid out for me.

> *24 got hit POWEE!!! right in the old snot locker.*
> *She fell down. That was not nice. If i knew a girl, i*
> *wudn't fight with her, no way hose-A!!*

"Norwood," I said, and tapped him on the shoulder. He looked at me, sneaked another peek through the telescope; then he sighed and bobbed his head and paid attention.

Our conversation had a disquieting air about it. I could imagine how horse trainers must feel. Good old Trigger was quiet and tame, but it was big and it had sharp hooves and the trainer could never be absolutely certain the horse wouldn't . . .

"Norwood, tell me what happened on this day." I held out his notebook and pointed to where he'd written about Twenty-four; Cricket's apartment number.

His lips moved as he slowly read it, then he nodded. "Oh, yeah, I remember. Pow! He really hit her."

"You say here, 'She fell down.' Was her face bleeding?"

Norwood's head bobbed rapidly. "Oh, yeah! Her nose, I think. A nosebleed. I used to get those and Mom would wrap ice in a towel and—"

"Okay, fine. Now, after he hit her, did he take a package away from her?"

Norwood shook his head. "Nah," he said.

"You're sure? Maybe he picked it up from her car seat. Did he reach into the car? Or did he get into the car for a minute?"

"Nah," said Norwood, "he didn't touch her car."

Hmm. Maybe there were only a few files and she had put them in her purse. "Well, he took her purse, didn't he?"

"Nah," Norwood said again, "he didn't take nothing."

That didn't make any sense.

"Norwood," I said calmly; forcing it, but calmly, "think carefully. You saw this guy hit Crick—uh, Twenty-four—on the nose."

Norwood nodded.

"But he didn't take anything from her. Not her purse or a package or an envelope or anything at all. Is that right?"

"Right!" Norwood said emphatically. "That's exactly positively right!"

"After he left," I said, "did anyone else come along and take anything from Twenty-four? Or from her car?"

Norwood hung his head. "Dunno," he said. "I didn't watch any more."

"Somebody hit her; she was lying on the ground bleeding; and you stopped watching? *Come on!*"

"Well, see, he Thirty-seven came home then and they started to—"

"Okay, okay," I said. "Then let's go back to the man who hit, uh . . . Twenty-four, damn it! The man who hit Twenty-four. Which way did he run?"

"Didn't run," Norwood said. "Got into his car."

Car? A mugger with a *car*? I had a sudden sick feeling. A book I once read had described that feeling as a "rush of shit to the heart."

I said, "Norwood, tell me what the man who hit Twenty-four looked like."

Norwood's face screwed up in concentration. "He's very handsome, like a movie star. He wears suits; you know, with ties and like that. And he has gray hair here, on his whatsits." Norwood flicked his fingers along his temples.

Hadley? Walter Worthless *Hadley*?

"Norwood, are you talking about Twenty-four's regular boyfriend? The man who used to visit her? Is *he* the one who hit her?"

"Yeah, sure. That guy." Norwood picked up his notebook and held it up close to his face with both hands.

"Didn't I put that in here?" he said.

CHAPTER THIRTY-SEVEN

I parked opposite Walter Hadley's fancy house and walked across the street. No, that's wrong. I didn't walk; I *stalked* across the street, thinking cold and furious thoughts about castration and dull razor blades.

As it turned out, he wasn't home yet. Ann Hadley told me that, standing in the front door with a quizzical look on her handsome square face. Then she looked past me and said, "Hang on, there's Walt now."

Hadley wheeled his Olds into the driveway as one of the ubiquitous Dormac-Chaffee Cavaliers snuggled against the curb. I didn't recognize either of the two men in the Cavalier. The Corporate Security division had a helluva manpower budget.

I went toward Hadley's car waving my arms and jabbering loudly. "About time, slugger! Hey, I was just telling Ann about the barbecue. Betty says . . ."

By then I was face-to-face with him as he got out of the car. "Hadley," I said in a lower voice, "I know you belted Cricket Dawes in that parking lot. Come into the house with me quietly, and your wife doesn't have to find out. Otherwise . . ."

He blanched. I turned toward the Cavalier and waved cheerfully. "How you doing there, boys?"

Hadley said, "All right, all right. I understand."

"What's with the company goons? And smile, damn it." I continued to beam at the Chevrolet.

"They're escorting me," Hadley said. "They say it's normal security procedure, but I wonder if . . ." He took a deep breath, reached back into the Olds for his briefcase, and we strolled toward his front door side by side. He even managed a lackluster wave to the goons. They didn't wave back.

We went inside. Ann Hadley slammed the front door and whirled on Walter. "Will you tell me what in the world is going on?"

I said, "Mrs. Hadley, is your daughter home?"

"No," she said, looking perplexed, "Jenny's spending the night with a friend. Why?"

"Does the name Cricket Dawes mean anything to you?"

"Wait a minute," Hadley said.

"Walt's secretary," his wife said. "The one who was killed. Or is there more?" Ann Hadley's eyes narrowed. She crossed her arms tightly and darted looks from Hadley to me and back again. She didn't like me, but the looks that landed on Hadley would have charred wallpaper.

"There's more," I said. "None of it is very pleasant, but since it's going to screw up your life for the next few years, maybe you'd better listen to it."

Hadley hurled his tooled leather briefcase at the wall. It dropped onto a hall table and broke a small pastel vase. "Goddamn it!" he said. "You promised you wouldn't—"

"Oh, get off it," I said. "You can't keep the lid on this anymore. Can't you see that?"

Ann Hadley's voice had a chilling tone. "Maybe he can't see, but I think I'm beginning to."

We sat in the Hadleys' formal living room, on brocade sofas behind marble-topped coffee tables. The lamps were brass-and-china with fabric shades, the wallpaper was richly flocked, and there were oil paintings on the walls. It was a very, very classy room.

To sit in that elegance and talk about what we talked about was jarring; like slaughtering hogs in an art gallery.

I wasn't as angry as I had been at first; my fury had all boiled down to a vague ache. I finally knew who gave Cricket the fatal nosebleed, and when I'd finished with Hadley, I'd know how and why.

And I hoped that I would find out who had the files. And I even hoped for more; I hoped to know how they got away with them. It never hurts to hope.

I pumped Walter about the details, but he kept going back over old ground to explain things to his wife. Finally I gave up and let him bleat away at her.

As bleaters went, he wasn't bad. His romance with Cricket had been a brief affair of the flesh; he'd been drunk the first time; he had never promised to marry her or anything like that; and he'd never do it again.

To which argument Ann Hadley replied, slowly and distinctly, "Bullshit."

Wally then claimed the mess wasn't his fault; the company was using him as a scapegoat because of missing files; Cricket was probably a Russian spy; and I was certainly an evil man seeking to destroy his wonderful marriage.

Ann Hadley thought that was bullshit, too.

Wally tried an off-the-wall approach next; a medley of: I can't go on without you; I only got into trouble because I worked hard for you and Jenny; and let's go away together, just you and I, when this is all over.

Ann: "Bullshit."

She rose gracefully. She seemed calm now, and purposeful.

"Wally old pal," I said, "methinks you're in deep shit."

Ann Hadley walked out of the room without a word.

"It appears to be my turn now," I said. "Let us review what you told me last time we chatted. This time, I want the unabridged version."

Hadley watched the doorway where Ann had disappeared. He nodded mechanically. "Go ahead," he said.

"You told me you caught Cricket making a list of which

files she wanted. You said that was a week before she was killed. To repeat a recent pungent phrase: bullshit. You caught her that Friday, didn't you?''

He nodded. ''I came out of my office about four-fifteen and found her putting confidential memos and reports into an expanding file; one of those accordion-pleated cardboard types.''

''I suppose the argument took place pretty much like you told me it did.''

''Yes,'' he said. ''She threatened to show Ann and the company the video if I stopped her. I couldn't do that, so she walked out with the files.''

Hadley fished around in his hip pocket and came up with a snowy ironed handkerchief. He wiped his eyes with it. ''At the office door Cricket stopped and looked back,'' he said. ''She was about to cry, I think, and she said, 'I didn't want it to end like this, Wally-bear.' Then she left.''

Walter Hadley sniffed loudly. ''Well, I didn't want it to end that way, either, but . . .'' He shrugged helplessly.

''Okay, so Cricket left the plant,'' I said, ''and you followed her. How far behind were you?''

''Not far,'' he said. ''Maybe three or four minutes out the gate, but I caught up. I was right behind her for the last couple of blocks. She didn't see me, though.''

''Until she got out of the car and you punched her.''

Hadley shook his head. ''No, it didn't happen that way. I tried to talk her out of it; I told her she couldn't get me back by blackmailing me with the files.'' He wiped his eyes again. ''I thought that's why she had taken them. I didn't know about the antinuke nuts until you told me that in the car last week.''

''Doesn't matter,'' I said. ''For whatever reason, you punched her.''

His voice had a dreamy undercurrent now. ''You know, I hadn't hit anyone since grade school, I think, but I just got so mad and so frustrated, I . . . I didn't realize I'd done it until I saw her fall down with blood coming out of her nose.

And my knuckles hurt." Absently he lifted his right hand to his mouth and sucked one knuckle as if the pain were still there.

"Where were the files?" I said. "Still in her car? Or was she holding them?"

Hadley shrugged. "In the car, I guess. I didn't see them."

"You sure you didn't take them?" Dumb question. If he had them, he wouldn't have tried to buy them from me. Still, very little else about this case made sense, so . . .

"No. I didn't take them." Hadley was dull and mechanically compliant. I had the feeling that if I asked him what color his blood was, he'd saw off an appendage to check.

"But why didn't you help her, Wally?" I said. "Why, for Christ's sake, did you go away and leave her to die?"

Wally looked directly at me for the first time. His eyes were hollow and haunted. "I don't know. I—I didn't think you could die from a bloody nose! Did you? I mean, goddamn, how can a *lousy bloody nose*—"

He put his hands over his face and went away to some lonely private place.

When he came back, he said, "Until you told me about that yesterday, I didn't know that's what had killed her. I swear. I knew I had given her a bloody nose, but I thought . . . A mugger . . . Or . . ."

He breathed in loudly and looked around his living room as if he'd never seen it before. "I didn't sleep last night," he said apologetically. "Can't eat, either. Won't stay down." He patted his stomach and tried to smile. "Crazy way to diet, huh?" The smile smeared and died away.

"One more thing," I said. "Until I stumbled across an eyewitness, you were in the clear because of that gate log at the plant; the one that showed you were still working when Cricket died. How did you manage that alibi?"

Hadley laughed goofily. "I didn't," he said. "It was that fool Polvinski. The gate guard. Ann had given his daughter some of Jenny's old clothes; Polvinski thought he owed me a favor. When he saw me leaving at four-thirty, he put down five-thirty instead. He told me the next day;

said he didn't want me to get into trouble for knocking off early!''

Hadley giggled then, a nasty giggle with a sharp, hysterical ring. It took a long time for the giggle to fade away. When it had, there was a soft noise. Ann Hadley stood in the doorway, watching us.

''Mr. Rafferty, can you give me a lift, please?'' Ice-maiden voice; bags and bags of control keeping the lid firmly clamped down.

I was generous; I gave Hadley a full ten seconds to say something. But he didn't, so I said, ''Sure,'' to his wife, and we left.

She had packed two suitcases; big leather ones with fabric inserts that got dirty when I put them in the trunk of the Mustang.

The Dormac-Chaffee goons watched us, alternating beady-eyed scrutiny with mystified glances at the Hadley house.

''Where to?'' I said when we were seated and the noises from under the Mustang's hood vaguely resembled a functioning automotive engine.

''That way,'' she said. ''It's not too far. I'll show you.''

I may have arched my eyebrows, or maybe she simply thought I deserved to know. ''The house where Jenny's staying. We'll get a cab to the airport from there.''

Her decision didn't surprise me.

She pointed out rights and lefts, and I made the turns. She asked me to stop beside a big brick barn of a place with two large elms in the front yard. I humped her suitcases onto the sidewalk and slammed the trunk.

''Leave the bags,'' she said, ''I'll get Bill to help. Just go. Please.''

I got into the Mustang and started it. She trotted quickly to the open passenger window. ''Wait, Mr. Rafferty.'' Her face was firm, but her eyes were wet as she asked the question. ''Walt . . . Walt did kill that girl, didn't he?''

I thought of a dozen convenient lies, then I finally said, ''Yes. He didn't mean to. Hell, he didn't even know he had done it until yesterday. But that's right, he killed her.''

She nodded twice, rapidly, and walked away.

As I pulled out from the curb, she marched up the sidewalk toward the brick house, her back straight and her handsome square chin held high.

CHAPTER THIRTY-EIGHT

I had only driven half a block from the house where Ann Hadley went for her daughter when the Dormac-Chaffee Cavalier wallowed and tire-squealed around a corner like it was late for the start of the Daytona 500.

There was a fair amount of pointing and arm waving in the Cavalier, a hurried U-turn, and then they settled in behind me, half a block back. *Who, us? We're just out for a drive.*

They stayed there all the way home, where I put the Mustang in my garage, sticky door or not. The Keystone Cops parked across the street and seemed to settle in for the long haul.

My service had messages. Winchester and Linda Taree. I didn't return either call.

I fixed and ate something—ham sandwiches, I think. Then I sat in the living room with the lights out and a bathtub-size Scotch in both hands.

I had a roaring case of the end-of-investigation megrims. I knew most of it now; how Cricket Dawes had died, how illogical the reasons were, how almost inevitable it had been from the first time she let Hadley smarm his way under her skin and into her bed.

But.

But what the hell happened to those files? Hadley didn't have them, Nagle didn't have them, I didn't have them, Winchester didn't have them. And there was no mugger anymore, so *he* didn't have them.

So who did?

Aaargh!

Around nine, I tried Hilda's hotel in St. Louis. She wasn't in her room. I hoped she would come back to Dallas soon. Then I thought about the goons outside, and I hoped she wouldn't come back soon.

I could hurt myself—one way or another—thinking too hard about things like that, so I poured another Scotch and turned on the television.

It came to life in the first third of an old movie. *Getaway*, with Steve McQueen and Ali McGraw. I'd seen it before. And read the book, too, in one of the several reprints since it was written way back whenever.

I watched the rest of *Getaway* and rooted for Steve and Ali as they were chased by the cops and two different sets of baddies.

While doing so, I drank a touch more Scotch than I'd planned.

At the end, when they bought the pickup from Slim Pickens and drove away into Mexico, I toasted Doc and his wife and wished them well.

I fell asleep on the couch then, and dreamed I was watching the movie again. This time it was a silent flick, and Billie the Kid was reading the player's lips. But the lines weren't the same. Ali McGraw had all the good speeches and McQueen was only a flunky.

Morning arrived early, and it had a big price tag on it. In addition to a painful throb behind my eyes, I paid dearly for not returning phone calls the night before.

Linda Taree showed up on my doorstep at seven. She followed me into the kitchen, where I started coffee perking and got out two cups. Then I croaked something back-in-a-minute-ish and went looking for aspirin, a shower, and clothes.

When I returned to the kitchen, the coffee was ready. Linda

had fried some bacon, too, and she had eggs at the ready. "Breakfast?" she asked brightly.

"Thanks," I said. "Three fried, with that jalapeño sauce on the shelf in the refrigerator door. What the hell are you doing here at this hour of the morning?"

"Now there's a change of pace," she said as she cracked eggs into the skillet one-handed. " 'Three eggs, please, and what the hell do you want?' What ever happened to 'good morning'?"

"Good morning. And speaking of changes of pace, what ever became of feminism? Won't you lose a merit badge or something for cooking my breakfast?"

"It's okay for me to cook it; it's not okay for you to *expect* me to cook it."

Since I had neither invited her to visit nor asked her to cook, it seemed to me that her response evaded the issue. Even so, I decided not to explore the topic any further just then. Maybe after a cup of coffee or two.

"Well, tell me about it," Linda said. "How goes the detecting business?"

I didn't want to even think about the Dawes case yet, let alone explain it to her. "Later," I said. "Play your cards right, you can watch a genuine detective at work."

She plunked a plate down in front of me and I groggily ate breakfast. And, unlikely volunteer or not, she was a pretty good cook.

Dormac-Chaffee was still on the job that Thursday morning. It was a different car—a green Oldsmobile Cutlass this time. The guys inside were new to me—again—and they looked a trifle seedier than normal. Still, overnight stakeouts do that to you.

They were enthusiastic, though, and when Linda and I left, they slotted in behind the Mustang like good little shadows.

A good breakfast, four cups of coffee, and another dose of aspirin had worn the sharp edges off my hangover. I felt downright frisky.

I led the Cutlass onto Central Expressway. "Und now," I

said to Linda Taree in my best Dr. Strangelove accent, "ve vill demonstrate how to remoof der unvanted tail."

I found a gap in the slow lanes and eased the Mustang into the fast lane beside the gap. An exit came up and finally—at the last possible second—I dove through the gap and up the exit ramp.

Behind us, brakes *squawp*ed and horns blared annoyance. As planned, the Dormac-Chaffee wonder boys didn't make the exit; they were swept past by the traffic.

Linda Taree laughed. "Aw-right! That's good!"

I turned left onto the overpass, left again, and slid down into the opposite-direction traffic on the other side of the expressway.

"By this time," I said, "they've turned around, but they're an exit or two back. So we do our little number again." I did, and cut it a tad too fine. A plumber's truck went up on two wheels when he swerved to miss us. "Just in case there's a second tail car we haven't identified."

I went back onto the expressway in our original direction. We saw the green Olds going the wrong way and waved to it. They got kind of excited about that.

One more slalom-style exit, and I turned away from the expressway. I let the Mustang drift through the back streets, vaguely headed for the Casa Cahuenga, while I mulled over the problem.

"Where are we going?" Linda asked.

"Shh." I tapped my temple. "Cogitation in progress."

Early in this case I'd bragged to Hilda about how easily I could prove things by disproving the alternatives; the Holmesian solution. So I should have been able to figure out where the files were. After all, I knew all the places they weren't. They weren't in Cricket's apartment, they weren't with Hadley, they weren't in Cricket's car. Trouble was, I couldn't think of what was left after I eliminated all of those.

Maybe I was wrong to eliminate the car. Hell, the cops weren't looking for files when they had searched the car. Maybe they missed something. Maybe I should warn Ed and Ricco.

First, though, I wanted one more look at the Casa Cahuenga.

Linda Taree fidgeted when I drove down the alley and pulled into Cricket's parking slot. "This is where she lived, isn't it?" she said. "Wow, spooky."

"Yeah, spooky. I'm going to wander around. You want to come along?"

She shook her head. Her springy hairdo wobbled for an instant after her face had stopped. "No, I'll just sit here. I wouldn't want to disturb you, Sherlock." She forced a bright laugh.

What the hell. Even Sherlock had his off days. I'd figure this thing out yet.

Maybe.

I mooched around the parking lot with my hands in my hip pockets for a while. Checked the dumpsters. Recently emptied; no help there. I poked around the back of the building, even chinned myself to examine the iron roof over a small padlocked storage lean-to. Nothing there, either.

I went through to the inner courtyard. It was past nine by then; the Casa Cahuenga was near deserted. I nodded hello to Stanley Mellish, the manager. He was headed out back with a big green plastic garbage bag.

I ambled around, feeling impotent, hoping a nice big juicy clue would run up and bite me on the ankle.

After a few minutes Mellish lumbered back. This time he stopped. "Now," he said, "I've got that out of the way. Do you want to get into the Dawes apartment again?"

"No," I said. "No, I'm afraid I'm finished there. Thanks anyway."

"Well, I just thought . . . Look, I know what that police sergeant said, but since you're here, it'll be all right. Cricket's sister can go in, if she wants."

"Cricket's sister," I said numbly.

"Sure. Thin girl with big red hair. She's out back. Isn't that your car?"

I beat Mellish to the parking lot by a dozen strides. Linda Taree looked up and smiled at me. Then Mellish came out, too, and Linda's smile turned to a grimace.

She wriggled across to the driver's seat of the Mustang and twisted the ignition key savagely, but she didn't know how sloppy that lock was and how you had to lift the key just a fraction while you turned it. She was still twisting and cursing when I got there, reached in, and pulled out the key. Then I opened the door and motioned her out of the car. "Let's have a little chat, sis."

Linda got out and stood with her head bowed. When I chunked the door shut, she shifted her weight suddenly and launched a full leg-swing kick at my crotch. I turned aside enough to catch it on the left thigh. She was wearing a pair of those semi-hard-soled, pointy-toed things made like boxing shoes. Her kick landed squarely on the big thigh muscle and hurt like hell. My leg went numb.

I couldn't take the chance she might run while I couldn't chase her, so I chopped her on the side of the head with the heel of my fist. She spun around and flopped over the hood of the Mustang.

Behind me, Mellish said, "Oh, my!"

A couple of minutes later, when her eyes had uncrossed, Linda Taree said a whole lot more than that.

CHAPTER THIRTY-NINE

"I was watching," Linda Taree said, "when Cricket drove in. I had a rental car parked in the next row, right up against the building."

We were sitting at a poolside table in the Casa Cahuenga courtyard. I'd persuaded Mellish to leave us alone for "the interrogation." I figured that was good for about twenty minutes of privacy; then he'd be back.

I could feel my leg again, and it seemed to work all right, so I didn't handcuff Linda to the heavy table, though it was a tempting thought.

Linda said, "Cricket got out of the car just as her boss, Hadley, stopped his car crossways behind hers. He went over to her and they talked. Argued, really. Anyway, pretty soon he hit her and she fell down. He left then, practically running for his car. So I went over and saw this big cardboard file-thing on the front seat of her car." Linda shrugged. "I took the files, then I left, too."

This stupid case just would not quit. The more I found out, the more confused I was.

"Wait a minute," I said. "If you took the files in the first place, why has Winchester been nagging me to find the god-damned things? Am I some red herring you two are trying to drag across the trail or what?"

205

She looked amused. "I don't work for Winchester. That dork can—"

"I know that. Now. But then, when you lifted the files—"

"No," she said, exasperated. "I *never* worked for Winchester, not really. The Green Army is a joke; I only joined them to keep an eye on what they were doing." She straightened her back proudly. "I belong to a real antinuclear force. We're new, but we're going to take over the fight and win! We're not weak, like—"

There was more, but I tuned it out. I was thinking about The Grape. He had it pegged all along, and I hadn't seen it. Jeez, what a dummy.

I interrupted Linda's sloganeering. "And the first step in this takeover was to steal any material Winchester came up with, right?"

She sniffed and looked away.

"What's the name of your group of brave and true social liberators, pray tell? The No, No, We Won't Glow Action Group?"

"Whatever you say, macho man," Linda said, grinning. She seemed contented, even elated, and I wondered why.

"Okay, then, you took the files to your group of anonymous do-gooders, and everyone had a good laugh about the smooth way you'd shafted silly Jim Winchester, right?"

After a few seconds she nodded. "Sure. And I kept working at The Green Army, especially after Winchester hired you. We wanted to know what you were up to."

"Why did you come back here posing as Cricket's sister?" I said.

She shrugged. "I couldn't pretend to be her mother, could I? See, we didn't know if those were the only files she'd lifted. Maybe her apartment was full of Dormac-Chaffee documents. If so, we wanted them all. That stupid fat man is a goody-goody, or I'd have gotten in. He believed I was Cricket's sister."

"Yeah," I said. "Cricket really has a sister, by the way."

Linda shrugged again. "Who cares?"

"Is that why you grabbed the files and ran, while Cricket was dying? Because you didn't care?"

She glared at me. "She was alive," she said. "She was choking, sort of, that's all!"

"She 'choked, sort of' to death, Linda, probably before you were even out of the parking lot."

"I know," she said, "and I felt bad about that. At first, especially. But when I thought about all the people and all the children threatened by lunatics like her with their nuclear—"

"You're talking about a secretary, for God's sake! She didn't know an atom from an orange peel."

Linda huffed and threw a dirty look at poor dumb world-blower-upper me.

Stanley Mellish appeared and stood by his office door. He watched us, shifting back and forth on his tree-trunk legs.

"Just one more thing," I said. My headache was nibbling at me again, and I felt logy. "Your interest in the last few days; the phone calls and sudden appearances at my house. You've been keeping tabs on me, right? Because something is about to happen."

Linda checked her watch. "It's happening right now. You're too late. We've won," she said with a triumphant sneer. "I don't have to be nice anymore."

Behind her, Mellish tentatively walked toward us.

Linda stood up. She was too proud to run; she wanted to make a showy exit. "Now, if you're through jerking off . . ."

I found myself both repelled and troubled by her. She was totally relaxed and confident now, cocooned and sustained by the righteous glow of her cause. Had she been like that from the beginning? Or had she evolved into it to rationalize her part in letting Cricket die? In either case, I hadn't seen it, and that lapse didn't help the rising taste of disgust in the back of my throat.

We looked at each other. Her eyes were big and green and chilling. They had the kind of look you'd expect to see in someone's eyes just before they go out on a roof to shoot pedestrians because "the voices told me to do it."

"Go," I growled. What can you say? Torquemada thought he was doing the right thing, too.

She curled her lip and turned to walk away. Stanley Mellish

was right behind her then, and she bumped into him. He made the mistake of grabbing her arm. "Hey, wait," he said. "Did Mr. Rafferty say you could—"

She slashed at him with one clawed hand, dragging long fingernails across his face. Mellish squeaked and let go of her. Linda strutted toward the front exit; Mellish stood rigid and stared while blood welled up in four parallel rips in his cheek.

Thirty feet away, Linda turned and called out, "Check out the TV news, macho man. And buy all the papers. You might learn something!" She laughed and went out to busy Gaston Avenue.

Mellish had a first-aid kit in his little office. While he got it out, I looked out the window and saw Linda hail a cab and climb in. Going to get her car at my place, I thought. Wonder if she'll burn down my house while she's there? Since she doesn't have to be nice anymore.

Mellish danced and sucked in air when I daubed iodine on his cuts and bandaged them. Then I went home. It seemed a very reasonable thing to take the rest of the day off.

When I got home, Linda's VW was gone, which wasn't surprising. But there was no sign of Dormac-Chaffee, either, and that was. The general rule when you lose contact is to wait at a place your subject frequents.

I figured they'd be around sooner or later, like bill collectors and the flu.

The phone was ringing as I unlocked the front door. I caught it before they gave up. "Hello."

"Oh, it's you," said a cool voice. It was Ramon, Hilda's antiques salesman. "Let me speak with her, please."

"Come on, Ramon," I said. "Hilda's in St. Louis, for God's sake."

"She's back," Ramon said. He sounded puzzled. "She left here an hour ago. She wanted to surprise you."

I said, "I'll tell her you called," and hung up.

Good news at last. Hilda probably stopped at her place to clean up. And perhaps pick up some of the fancy underwear from San Antonio? I wondered if my *guayabera* was clean.

I thought of Linda Taree's crack about the news and turned on the television. Maybe there would be a midday newscast.

The screen lit up with what seemed to be a live news conference. A stocky bearded man sat behind a brightly lit table with a mound of documents in front of him. He held up two or three pieces of paper and talked loudly. He had a nasal New York accent.

". . . shows that for a period of at least thirty-two hours, residents around the plant were exposed to excessive radiation in the form of particulate contamination, following the failure of an improperly maintained HEPA filter."

Ho boy, I thought. Now it was obvious why Dormac-Chaffee had laid off me, and probably everyone else. They had all the trouble they could handle at the moment; they couldn't afford to get caught harassing the citizenry.

Hilda had timed it just right with her homecoming. Good work, babe, I thought. Hurry along now.

On the screen the bearded man kept talking, but the station cut back to the newsroom. A Very, Very, Serious Daytime Talking Head glanced sideways to check his profile in the monitor, then looked straight out at all of us in televisionland. VVSDTH had a deep, resonant voice and thought himself exceeding handsome.

"More details from that ongoing news conference throughout the day. In other news from the antinuclear movement, it's been a gloomy Thursday morning for another Dallas group, The Green Army."

The screen changed to a burned-out building. The camera lingered lovingly while firemen kicked apart a pile of rubble and hosed it down. Then there was a tight shot of Winchester, gaunt and worried, his mouth moving silently as he talked to someone off camera.

VVSDTH said, "The Dallas office of The Green Army was totally destroyed in a predawn fire. Green Army founder and president Dr. James Winchester has alleged arson. The fire is being investigated by the arson squad, but there's no report yet. And . . ."

VVSDTH paused significantly before the next item. My

phone rang at the same time. I backed up, reaching for the
phone while watching the television.

VVSDTH put on his solemn face and said, "The body of
a Dormac-Chaffee executive was found at his luxury home
this morning, the victim of an apparent suicide. Walter Hadley, head of Dormac-Chaffee's . . ."

Well, goddamn, I thought. I fumbled for the phone, said
"Hold on a minute," into the receiver and put it down on
the table. It squawked angrily behind VVSDTH's dulcet
tones.

". . . garage, with a hose from the exhaust leading into
the car. Dormac-Chaffee officials dismissed as 'ridiculous'
suggestions that Mr. Hadley committed suicide because of
discrepancies claimed in today's startling news conference
concerning . . ."

I put the phone to my ear. "Yo."

It was Elmo Nagle, his voice cold and menacing. "We got
your girlfriend, hoss."

CHAPTER FORTY

Something clamped down hard in my chest. I don't know what a heart attack feels like, but it couldn't be far from that sudden fierce squeeze.

Oh, my God, Hil, honey, I've been gawping at television while Nagle's greaseballs—

Nagle chuckled evilly. "Lifted her right out of that little Kraut car, slick as you please." I decided to kill him the instant Hilda was safe.

"You didn't call to brag," I said, carrying the phone to the closet. "Say it, Nagle. Tell me what you want." I held the phone with my shoulder while I pulled weapons out of the closet.

The Ithaca twelve-gauge, I'd definitely need that, and maybe the sawed-off, too. It depended on—

"I want you, old hoss," Nagle said. "In the flesh, as they say. After I've got you . . . why, then we'll talk about what else I'm gonna get for this broad."

"Sure," I said, "that's okay. When and where?" I had a full box of double aught buckshot somewhere; wouldn't want to forget that. And the ankle holster, for a backup gun. Now where did I put that bulletproof vest?

"You're too cute, Rafferty," Nagle said. "You shit-house rat. And you're too close to Durkee and his pal. I'll call you back from a different phone. Ten minutes. Be there.'' He hung up.

I dialed Cowboy's number immediately. He didn't waste time asking questions. ''Mimi and me'll be there soon as we kin,'' he said. ''You want Jim and Andy, too?''

''Too early to tell,'' I said. ''I don't know how he wants to set up the meet.''

''I'll get 'em started,'' Cowboy said. ''It don't hurt to be ready. Now you jest relax, Rafferty, we gonna get her out okay.''

''Yeah. Make it snappy, will you?''

''We're rolling now,'' he said.

I hung up and checked three times that the receiver was properly seated. This was no time for Nagle to get a busy signal.

I piled all the weaponry I could possibly need on the kitchen table and sorted through it. An old double-barreled sawed-off shotgun I'd taken off someone years ago was dry and dusty. I stripped it down and got out the cleaning kit and oil.

My hands were oily and I almost dropped the phone when it rang after an eternity that had lasted exactly eight minutes by my watch.

It was Nagle.

''Okay, hoss,'' he said, ''here's the way we gonna do it. You remember Fulvio's.''

It wasn't a question, but I answered it anyway. ''Fulvio's. Got it.''

Someone fumbled with the front door. Damn! Cowboy and Mimi were quick. I clamped a hand over the mouthpiece and called, ''It's open. Come in.'' Then I said into the phone, ''Right. Fulvio's. Okay.''

Half of my mind plotted killing zones from that opening in Fulvio's back fence. Say, Mimi with her Uzi, and—

''Four o'clock sharp,'' Nagle said, ''and you'd better be alone or . . .''

''For the price of a BMW,'' said my favorite voice from the front door, ''you'd think they'd give you one that wouldn't get a flat tire!''

Hilda stalked in, her business-lady suit dirty and rumpled, her hands gray, and a smear of grease on the tip of her terrific nose. She looked at the guns and she looked at me. "Rafferty, what . . . ?"

I finally began to think. Nagle couldn't know about Hilda. So who had he—

"Wait a minute," I said to the phone. "I'm a pretty popular guy. Exactly which girlfriend did you snatch?"

Hilda came forward and stood beside my chair. I put my arm around her waist.

"Who do you think, hoss?" Nagle roared. "The redhead. Who else shows up on your doorstep before breakfast?"

I felt like a cartoon character when the light bulb goes on over his head. Dormac-Chaffee gave up sometime in the middle of the night; the green Cutlass had been Nagle's goons. They *did* come back to the house, and they grabbed Linda Taree after she retrieved her car. And a VW was a "little Kraut car," too, just like a BMW.

"Oh, that one," I said. "Her, you can have."

Nagle spluttered. In the background I thought I heard Linda yelp angrily, but that may have been wishful thinking. Hilda and I held hands.

"Hey, Nagle, I have a question for you. Did you ever read an O. Henry short story called 'The Ransom of Red Chief'?"

"No," he said, "of course not, why—"

"I think you're going to be sorry about that," I said.

I dropped the phone onto its cradle, stood up, and kissed Hilda for a long time.

"Maybe I will go to St. Louis with you sometime," I said, "if only to visit the restaurants."

"Restaurants?" she said. The grease smudge on her nose was the cutest thing I'd seen in years.

I kissed her again. "Well, it must be the St. Louis food," I said. "I can't remember you ever tasting this good before."

ABOUT THE AUTHOR

W. GLENN DUNCAN, a former newsman and profes-
sional pilot, has lived in Iowa, Ohio, Oregon, Florida,
Texas, and California. He now lives with his wife and
three children in Australia. His previous novels are
RAFFERTY'S RULES and RAFFERTY: LAST SEEN
—ALIVE.

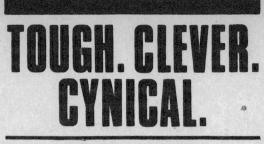

TOUGH. CLEVER. CYNICAL.

*An ex-cop, a deadly shot,
a man who plays by his own rules.......*

W. GLENN DUNCAN'S:

RAFFERTY